THE FIGHT FOR MIDNIGHT

DAN SOLOMON

flux

Mendota Heights, Minnesota

First Edition
First Printing, 2023

Book design by Cynthia Della-Rovere
Cover design by Cynthia Della-Rovere
Cover illustration by Chloe Zola

Flux, an imprint of North Star Editions, Inc.

Library of Congress Cataloging-in-Publication Data
Names: Solomon, Dan, 1980- author.
Title: The fight for midnight / Dan Solomon.
Description: First edition. | Mendota Heights, Minnesota : Flux, 2023. |
    Audience: Grades 10–12.
Identifiers: LCCN 2022061119 (print) | LCCN 2022061120 (ebook) | ISBN
    9781635830866 (hardcover) | ISBN 9781635830873 (ebook)
Subjects: CYAC: Interpersonal relations--Fiction. | Abortion--Fiction. | Bullies
    and bullying--Fiction. | LCGFT: Novels.
Classification: LCC PZ7.1.S6689 Fi 2023 (print) | LCC PZ7.1.S6689 (ebook) |
    DDC [Fic]--dc23 LC record available at https://lccn.loc.gov/2022061119
LC ebook record available at https://lccn.loc.gov/2022061120

Flux
North Star Editions, Inc.
2297 Waters Drive
Mendota Heights, MN 55120
www.fluxnow.com

Printed in Canada

For Will, Griffin, Cooper, Eli, Aidan, Ben,
Hal, Julian, Charlie, and
all of the boys who will
need to show up.

9:03 am

'm running late when my phone rings. I was supposed to be inside the Austin Adult Day Care Center, where the terms of my deferred prosecution have me doing community service all summer, three minutes ago. But my phone never rings these days, so I answer the call out of curiosity. "Hello?"

"Hi! Is this Alex Collins?" a friendly—downright bubbly, even—female voice asks me.

"It is," I say, pressing the phone to my ear with my shoulder as I lock my bike to the rack outside the center.

"Hey, Alex. It's Cassie," she says, then adds for clarification, "Ramirez."

If I had any friends left, I would assume this is a prank from someone who knows about my lifelong crush on Cassie Ramirez. But I haven't had any friends in months. I have no idea why Cassie Ramirez would be calling me, or even where she got my number, but I don't have time to ask for the details. I can't afford to get into trouble for blowing off community service, so I just stammer, "Hey, Cassie," and head toward the door.

"What are you doing later today?" she asks me, like that's a normal question for her to ask me, like the fact that we haven't exchanged more than half a dozen words since we were in fourth grade would naturally lead to a morning phone call on a Tuesday in the summer.

"Um—I'm not sure," I say. "No plans yet."

That's an understatement. The theme of my Summer of 2013 has been "no plans yet," starting basically from the day school let out until this very moment, where my only plan consists of reading fifty pages of a gruesomely violent fantasy series to a man in his eighties who always wants more of the beheadings.

"I'm really glad to hear that," she says, then laughs a disarming, self-conscious laugh. "I mean, no offense. But today is really important. You should come to the Capitol as soon as you can. There's a lot going on, and you could really help out."

"At the Capitol? Like a bake sale or something?" I ask, still waiting outside the center.

"Like a protest," she says. "A big one. And I really need your help. Can you be there?"

Cassie's popular, so if she's calling *me*, she must

be trying to build the biggest army of protesters of all time. I didn't even know she cared about politics. But it's safe to assume that right now, she's calling everybody she hasn't already texted, Facebooked, tweeted, tagged on Instagram, Snapchatted, or re-blogged on Tumblr in order to rally the troops. I deleted all of that stuff a few months ago, which is probably why she's on the phone with me.

So this isn't Cassie revealing that she's also had a secret crush on me for forever, but that's okay. The summer before your senior year is supposed to be the best time of your life, but mine has just been lonely. Not only is Cassie the prettiest girl in school, but she's also one of the nicest—even to me and the people I used to hang out with, when plenty of other people just saw us as weirdos. It's not like I'm busy, and who knows? Showing up when she says she needs my help can't be a *bad* way to spend time with her. I tell her that she can count on me. I'm in.

"That's so great! Text me when you get here, okay? I'll be somewhere in the rotunda," she says, "wearing blue."

* * *

The halls of the Austin Adult Day Care Center are musty, but the place is nicer than you'd expect from the outside. "Adult day care" is basically what it sounds like—for elderly people whose grown children care for them at home, it's a place they can be during the day. It's complete with nursing staff, activities to do, and healthy meals they can eat without running the risk of setting the kitchen on fire—awesome if you're an octogenarian, less cool if you're seventeen. But at least it gets me out of the house. If you've got only one friend who isn't your mom, it doesn't matter too much if he's eighty-five years old and spends his days in a stuffy building with linoleum floors.

When I came in for my first day of community service, the lady who coordinated the visit told me Mr. Monaghan couldn't see very well, and it might be nice for someone to read to him. She promised that they had plenty of books to choose from. But when I got here, all I could find was a dusty shelf with every *Da Vinci Code* book and an unofficial sequel to *Gone with the Wind*. I asked Mr. Monaghan which he'd prefer, and he made a gagging noise.

"You look like a reader. You got anything in that purse of yours?" he asked, gesturing to my messenger bag.

I did, in fact, have a copy of *A Game of Thrones* on me, and I told him so.

"That's the one they make that television program about with the dragons, isn't it?" he asked. "Is it good?"

I'd only started *reading* it——we used to all get together every Sunday to watch the show at Jesse's house, at least until the most recent season——but as lonely as this summer was shaping up to be, I figured I'd be able to get through five doorstoppers of a fantasy series.

"Yeah," I said. "I'm not very far along, but so far——I like it."

He asked if I minded starting back at the beginning, and I told him I was there solely to amuse and entertain him. I read him the first fifty pages that day, and Mr. Monaghan was *into it*. I've been back three mornings a week since, and we're more than halfway through now. He made me promise not to read ahead without him, and I've kept my word. And whenever things get dicey in the book, he gets more and more enthusiastic. In some ways, it really is a lot like watching the show at Jesse's, where waiting for the show on Sunday nights felt like our group's version of watching sports.

"There's our man!" Mr. Monaghan says as I make my way into the smallish room we meet in. He's sitting in one of the armchairs against the wall, his thin, lanky frame draped over it like an old coat and his eyes half-closed. He's wearing a gray-and-brown flannel shirt——as ugly a shirt as you're likely to find——like a jacket over a black-and-red flannel shirt, which he's got buttoned up. Sometimes, it's impossible to tell if Mr. Monaghan does the things he does solely to mess with you.

"Yep! Sorry I'm late." I set my bag down on top of the old piano in the corner of the room and take a seat in the other armchair.

"It's a hot one out there, isn't it? And you're on a bike. Shit," he says, which is the sort of thing he says a lot——he was a sailor in World War II. "I'm lucky you keep coming at all."

"It's not totally up to me," I say. "But I wouldn't miss it anyway."

"Oh, that's right, you're a delinquent," he says with a laugh. "I forgot about that."

"I wish I could," I say.

"You're on deferred prosecution. Nobody besides me will ever even know."

Mr. Monaghan doesn't know that the brief flirtation with delinquency that led me to my role as his reading buddy is the least of my problems, and I don't really want him to. So I change the subject. "Want to catch up with what's happening in King's Landing?"

"Hell yeah." He smiles.

I crack the book, and things are easy for the next hour or so. I can't stop myself from doing the character voices to try to sound like the actors on the show.

Fortunately, Mr. Monaghan stopped making fun of how awful my British accents are a few weeks back, otherwise we'd never make any progress in the book. Fifty-three pages later, I tuck *A Game of Thrones* back in my bag.

"You staying cool out there this summer? It's a hot one today. Stay indoors if you can," Mr. Monaghan says. "I wouldn't put a dog out there in this fucking heat."

"I'll do my best," I say. "I'm not sure if they have air-conditioning at the Capitol."

"The Capitol?" he asks. "Why the hell are you going to that shithole?"

Before I can even answer, I find myself blushing. Am I really about to hang out with Cassie Ramirez?

"There's a protest today," I say. Feeling bold, I add, "A girl invited me."

"Hell, good for you," he says. "To a protest at the Capitol? Give 'em hell. Is this about the abortion thing?"

I realize that I have no clue what we're protesting. It didn't even occur to me to ask. Abortion. I think I saw something about that on the news. There were lots of people yelling at each other.

"Yup," I say, even though I'm not totally sure.

"What they're doing is fucked up," he says, and I nod. Then I remember that he probably can't see me.

"It is," I say quietly, embarrassed of my ignorance. I mean, I guess abortion is a bad thing? My mom is Catholic—like Cassie's family is—so I know that the priests and my mom don't like it. But most Sundays, I tell her that I'll ride my bike to the late-morning mass so I can sleep in, then I go to the coffee shop across the street to read for an hour instead. So I can't say that I've spent a lot of time listening to the priests lately.

"Say hi to Debbie if you see her down there," Mr. Monaghan says, referring to his daughter. Debbie Monaghan is the reason I started coming here, as opposed to doing my court-mandated hours any-where else. She's a friend of my mom's from church. When my mom confided to her that I needed to find a volunteer position, she mentioned that her dad was coming here now, and he could use someone to keep him company since he didn't take to the staff very well.

"I didn't know she was going," I say.

"Yeah, she's been there all week, since this bull-shit started," he says. "She took the day off work today to help organize people. It's important, what you're doing."

"It is." I nod, suddenly feeling a rush of conviction.

This past school year, I did a lot of things I regret. Reading to Mr. Monaghan makes me feel a bit better, because it means I must not be a *complete* asshole. I don't know exactly what the protest is all about, but Debbie is super nice, a total moral compass, so if she'll be at the Capitol, then going there is another chance for me to be a decent person, too—and if it happens to mean that I end up spending a few hours this afternoon hanging out with the prettiest girl in Austin, Texas, I guess I'll just consider that a bonus. As far as all the abortion stuff goes, I haven't really thought about it much—but I'm a guy, so why *would* I?

10:17 am

After I say goodbye to Mr. Monaghan, I slide my headphones out of my pocket and put them in my ears even though my mom, who's a safety nut, would kill me if she knew. I get on my bike and pedal my way toward the Capitol like a man making a jailbreak. I used to ride this route pretty much every day back when I had friends, so I know that doing so today is going to mess with me. I put on a country album my mom used to play on road trips when I was a kid—something nobody I know listens to, that won't remind me of anything from the past year—and power my way up the hill, past the colorful houses with big porches and old trees in their front yards.

I'm listening to Willie Nelson sing about how you can't hang a man for killing a woman who's trying to steal your horse when I see Jesse's house to my right. It's been months, but I can still see little flecks of broken glass along the curb that probably got swept over there and that nobody will ever clean up. And because I can't resist, I crane my neck as I pass by his mom's Volvo for a glimpse of the garage apartment behind the house. I learned before I deleted my Facebook account that it had been rented to a college student.

Of course, Jesse's not there, which makes me want to pedal my bike 100 miles per hour, preferably up to the moon. But that's not any more possible than seeing him sitting on the patio with his laptop, so I just focus on the music and the tale of the Red Headed Stranger and ride faster through the University of Texas campus on my way downtown.

The campus is mostly empty, which makes sense for the summer. That makes it an especially rude surprise when, as I ride past the football stadium, I catch a glimpse of Jacob Kohler's shaved head, striped polo shirt, and thick linebacker's body.

What the hell is he doing there? But then I realize—he must be taking summer classes, which means that he's going to UT and not Northwestern like he'd planned. I duck my head, blow the stop sign, and speed past all the college students so that he doesn't see me, since I'm sure if he's stuck going to college in Austin, he blames me for it. If I actually prayed, I'd say a prayer right now that it's the last time I'll ever see him, but praying is not something I do. So I pour all of that energy into fleeing him and the UT campus instead, clearing a route I've ridden a million times before with fresh urgency.

* * *

OCTOBER OF SOPHOMORE YEAR

I was getting ready to clock out at Double Dave's PizzaWorks when I heard Jacob Kohler's voice behind me. "What's up, Collins? Big plans tonight?"

Jacob was a year ahead of me at school and not someone I'd choose to hang out with, but he was a pizza maker and I worked the ovens. That means we spent a fair amount of time together at the part-time job I got as soon as I turned sixteen. I quickly learned how confounding he could be: a total asshole most of the time, but then surprisingly cool just often enough that you'd put up with him when he was being a jerk. When we both closed with Arno, our manager, Jacob would be chill and normal, especially if we talked about something we all cared about, like Marvel movies or our dogs. When we were on a busy weekend evening shift, and we had a full staff making sure every University of Texas party had a huge stack of pizzas at the ready, he would comfortably assume the center of attention and command the kitchen with his booming voice, offering a "Pick up the pace!" to a pizza maker who was saucing pies too slowly and a "Nice one" to another who could really sling the pepperoni down. And then, on nights like this one, when it was just the two of us, he'd be a crapshoot—he might offer to put my bike in the back of his truck and give me a ride home, or he might make fun of all of my friends, whose very existence he seemed to take as an affront. I braced myself to see which Jacob I was going to get tonight.

"Well?" he said with a smirk. "You gonna go get laid?"

I slipped the punch card into the ancient time clock the restaurant had probably had since 1996. It made a satisfying *ca-chunk* noise as it stamped the time—just after midnight—on the card. I didn't know what to say. He was definitely doing that thing where someone makes fun of you while pretending it's an innocent question. I stepped out of the way so he could clock out and pretended like I didn't hear him.

He kept going: "Me and some boys got a poker game tonight. You want in?"

It was weird that Jacob Kohler was inviting me to do *any*thing, but probably he and his friends just wanted to take all of my money.

"Maybe next time," I said. "Thanks, though."

When I got outside, I texted my best friend, Jesse, to find out where he was. I'd already told my mom that I'd be staying at his house that night, but Jesse's mom was super permissive about letting us stay out late and go to shows and stuff, so I didn't know if he'd be home or out with some of our other friends at an all-night diner or something.

He texted back immediately: *Hey! Can you meet us downtown?* with capital letters and punctuation because he was going to be a writer and decided that stuff was important. The ride downtown from Double Dave's wasn't far, so I texted back *sure*, unlocked my bike, strapped the headlight to the handlebar, and started pedaling.

There isn't much to do in downtown Austin when you're sixteen, unless there's an all-ages show at the Mohawk, so I didn't know what to expect. Jesse sent me a pin on his phone, and I followed it to the Texas State Capitol building, which I hadn't been to since the last time we'd gone for a middle school field trip.

I met Jesse in fifth grade, after my dad left and I switched from an expensive Catholic school to public school. Jesse was the first friend I made. He saw me reading *The Lord of the Rings* at lunch, and we started talking about hobbits. Pretty soon I spent so much time at his house that his mom told me I should "think of this as your home, too." That was great for both me and my mom—she worked extra hours then, and sending me to Jesse's when I was eleven was cheaper than getting a babysitter, and a lot more fun.

I made my way up the big hill on Brazos Street and turned right to get to the Capitol. The grounds were always well lit at night, and it looked kind of magical, how bright it could be even though it was dark out. I saw Jesse, his girlfriend, Shireen, and her friend Holly checking out a sculpture of something or other, and I walked my bike over. When they saw me coming, the three of them immediately began posing like the person in the sculpture, a random bit of goofiness that made me smile and also feel a tinge of regret. An hour earlier, Jacob had talked trash about Jesse's black nail polish and Shireen's art project where she made collages of famous athletes as Disney princesses, and I'd said nothing to stop him.

"Check this out," Jesse said when I got close to the statue. It was a guy on horseback with a rifle in his hand. "They still have statues of Confederate soldiers up here."

Shireen flipped it off. "Can we go get some eggs?"

"Only if we want to go to jail for a thousand years," Holly said. She was right that there were cops around who wouldn't look kindly on vandalizing a statue—even one that totally deserves it—but somehow it felt like we were the only people at the Capitol that night. "You smell like pizza," she added, looking at me.

Holly and I weren't really friends, even though I think Jesse and Shireen wanted us to hit it off.

Jesse nodded. "Hell yes, he does," he said, before giving me a big hug and inhaling deeply. "Glorious, glorious pizza."

Shireen snorted and pointed to a state trooper in a big cowboy hat who was watching Jesse's public display of affection with a wary eye. In response, Jesse grabbed all of us—me and Shireen and Holly—into an enormous group hug.

"We're being driven to amorous activity by the sight of Jefferson Davis, Officer!" he called. Shireen burst out laughing, and then we all cracked up. The trooper shook his head and kept making his rounds.

Jesse loved doing stuff that made stodgy conservative people—the kind you couldn't escape from if you lived in Texas, even in Austin—do a double take. Which was one of the reasons we were friends and, I supposed, one of the reasons he and Jacob Kohler weren't.

"Can you guys believe that Austin City Limits is happening right now and we're not there?" I said, eager to fully change the subject to something other than the aroma of pepperoni and tomato sauce I was still carrying with me.

"Unbelievable! This is absolutely the last time

we'll let that happen," Jesse declared. "Next year, we'll be there for sure."

I looked out at my friends, on the lit-up grounds of the Capitol—this expansive space that even the patrolling state troopers didn't make feel any less ours. In that moment, thinking about next year and the music festival and who'd be playing and how we'd be there, everything felt limitless.

10:27 am

The Capitol grounds take up four square blocks of downtown Austin. At the center is an enormous structure, a pinkish limestone building that looks like the US Capitol but is actually *bigger* (a point of pride in Texas). Surrounding the building are sidewalks and paths for people to walk on, entrances that lead to subbasements and extension buildings, and one of the nicer grass lawns in drought-starved Austin.

In my memory, the Capitol is a sleepy old building with a big, empty lawn, but today, there are people *everywhere.*

There are protesters, state troopers, and police officers on horses. I ride my bike past women waving signs and groups chanting slogans. I slow my roll to see one big sign reads "My Body, My Choice!" while the next one over reads "Kill the Bill." A person with long hair and a *V for Vendetta* mask holds a sign that reads "Abort Rick Perry," referring to the governor of Texas.

I yank out my headphones because I can barely hear the music with all the noise. Without them in, I hear a big group by the steps of the building chant, "Not the church, not the state, women must decide our fate!" Down closer to the street, another group shouts, "When women's rights are under attack, what do we do? Stand up, fight back!"

As I slow to a stop, it suddenly dawns on me that there are *two* sides to this whole "protest" thing that Cassie invited me to.

As I look around, it's surprisingly easy to figure out who's who. The protesters are color coded, wearing uniforms like they're here to cheer for two different football teams. The people waving signs and chanting about women's rights wear orange clothes, and the other people—the ones giving them dirty looks—wear blue. Like Cassie said she would be. That tracks with what I know about her, which is that she is the most Catholic girl on the planet who isn't an actual nun.

I lock my bike to a tree and walk toward the building. It all reminds me of going to UT football games with my dad, which brings up a whole other set of things I don't want to think about, so I shake my head fast like I'm trying to reboot my brain.

I've only been inside the Capitol for class field trips, but it's not hard to pick out the entrance: it's the one with the long, snaking line of people, most of whom are wearing orange. I try to do a rough crowd count, grouping people two by two, before I realize that it's impossible. There are fifty people ahead of me in line, and we make up only a tiny, tiny fraction of the people who are here on the grounds. There have got to be hundreds, if not thousands, with the orange ones outnumbering the blue ones. No wonder Cassie dug so deep on people she knew and called me.

The crowd is mixed—men and women, young and old, white and Black and Hispanic and more. As I walk inside, I spot a couple of older guys in short-sleeved blue button-up shirts and ties. One of them has a goatee and a hand-held video camera, and he's filming people in orange. They don't seem to be bothering anybody, but the people in orange react like he's pointing a gun at them.

"Get that thing out of my face," a lady in her fifties yells at him. "You people are trying to steal our rights. At least respect my right not to be filmed."

The guy walks backward toward a group of blue-shirts who are all singing "Amazing Grace" at the top of their lungs, his camera still trained on the people in orange. A girl in orange who's maybe a little older than me finally sprints over to him, looks right into the lens, and screams "Hail Satan!" Camera Guy turns to his friend, who also speaks directly to the lens, saying, "The cheerleaders of death have spoken for their master!"

As for me, I've never been more grateful to be wearing a white T-shirt, even if it's drenched in sweat.

The line for the metal detector is short and moves quickly. I watch as one guy in a suit walks up behind me, passing the line, and flashes an ID card to the public safety officer.

"CHL," the man in the suit says.

"Go ahead," the security officer replies.

The woman in front of me in line, maybe a little younger than my mom and wearing an orange shirt, shakes her head at this. "Unbelievable," she says.

"What happened?" I ask.

"A CHL is a concealed handgun license. We're going through metal detectors every time we go in and out, and that guy just walked in packing a gun," she explains.

I guess that lady hasn't been in Texas long, if she's surprised by that, but I just shrug and make a noise that I hope sounds like I mean "Yep, that sure is weird or whatever," before I empty my pockets and pass through the metal detector.

After grabbing my phone from the tray, I text Cassie to let her know that I'm here.

Great, she texts back. *Who is this?*

My heart sinks, but I guess it makes sense. How

many calls and texts must she have made this morning before she got to me, of all people? I text her
back to identify myself and ask where to meet her.
She responds quickly, informing me that she's in a
line on the third floor of the rotunda.

"Excuse me," I say to a lady in orange who's
staring intently at her phone. "Do you know where
the rotunda is?"

She spreads her arms wide and spins a little, like
she's pointing to the entire planet. "You know that
round dome thing you saw when you looked at the
building from outside? That's the rotunda. You're
in it."

That clears that up. I find the nearest set of stairs.
It's tough to get up the staircase because there are
so many people on it. It's like trying to pass through
the halls at school when everybody is going to lunch.
I try to make myself as narrow as I can and push
my way up.

When I get to the third floor, I look for where
Cassie and all the rest of the kids she wrangled together must be hanging out. Instead, I see a group in
orange holding signs and banners that read "Stand
with Texas Women." They're surrounding a group
of guys in blue—some probably my age, or close to
it—who have red duct tape with the word *LIFE*
written on it over their mouths. They've got the same

thing on the palms of their hands, which they hold up at 45-degree angles from their shoulders.

Seeing these guys makes me miss Jesse a lot. If he were here, he'd see the same thing I do—this pose looks a *lot* like the "Sieg Heil" salute you see in pictures of Nazi Germany. It makes me wonder what Jesse would have made of all this, if this had been going on back when we were still friends. It's not like we would just hang out and talk about abortion after lunch. But I push that question out of my mind, which I've gotten good at doing whenever I find myself thinking about Jesse.

I can't believe there are so many people here. This is what people do on Tuesdays in the summer, I guess—they put on color-coded shirts, stick tape over their mouths, make signs, and get all of their friends to come down here even though it's approximately one million degrees outside, all so they can scream at strangers. For me, it beats spending yet another afternoon at home by myself, but even if the alternative weren't boring as hell—and even if I weren't psyched about the fact that I'm about to hang out with Cassie Ramirez—it's exciting to be around all this action.

I brush past the mouth-tape LIFE dudes and finally see Cassie's long black hair and golden-brown skin. She looks totally stunning in her short-sleeve, knee-length blue dress, even though she's standing with her head down and her eyes trained on her phone. To my surprise, she's surrounded by people in orange. Where are all of her friends?

10:43 am

walk past the assembled oranges over to Cassie and say, "Hey," like that's a killer opening line. But she smiles big.

"Hey!" she says back. Then she throws her arms around me like we hug all the time. I freeze up, then pat one hand on her shoulder, real cool-like, before she disengages.

Smooth, Alex.

"Thank you so much for coming," she says as she stuffs her phone back into her purse. She seems relieved for the company. Being the only one in blue over here has to be hard.

"I hope you don't think you're cutting the line," a voice says behind me. I turn to see three people—a guy probably in his twenties and two women—all wearing orange and glaring at me. The guy adds, "People have been here for hours waiting to get in." I glance down the hall and realize that in my zeal to find Cassie, I walked past a line that snakes down the stairs and all the way around to the ground floor.

Cassie rolls her eyes at me real quick, then smiles. "Of course not, sir," she says. "He's just saying hello."

The guy huffs, folds his arms, and turns back to his group.

"Holy crap," I whisper to Cassie. "This is all nuts, right? Like, that's not a normal thing for a person to do."

"Oh my gosh, it's *bananas*," she says. "I've been here for the last two hearings. It's been absolutely nuts."

"Are you—like—are you doing this by yourself?"

"Yeah." She nods. "I mean, mostly. My dad and my stepmom have been here for some of it, but they have work today. And there are some other people from church, but—it's hard to get people to spend a nice summer day doing something important instead of, like, swimming at Barton Springs or something."

"Right."

"But you're here. I knew *you* would come," she says.

She did? I have no idea why she would think that, but the fact that Cassie thought anything about me at all is pretty dang flattering.

I don't know what to say, so I just mumble, "I'm sure more people will come."

She laughs and shakes her head. "I don't think so.

It's just you and me. But you've always been there for me when I've needed you."

This is starting to get weird—like, maybe Cassie has me confused with a different Alex or something. Did she think she was texting some other kid? But no, I'm right here, she gave me a hug, and she is looking right at me, so she definitely didn't expect someone else to show up. Or maybe she did, and she's just so effortlessly classy and cool that she's pretending not to be surprised? Man, she's amazing.

She smiles and gently puts her hand on my forearm. "You don't remember, do you? I guess that makes sense. It couldn't have meant as much to you as it meant to me. But when we were in fourth grade, back at St. Gabriel's—do you remember?"

Of course I remember. I just can't believe that she does.

I went to St. Gabriel's from kindergarten through fourth grade. Cassie stayed all through middle school, though. Even back then, we were different kinds of kids—Cassie was popular immediately, and I hid away at lunchtime, trying to find a place I could draw in peace. But she was also the kid who, when her mom made her bring valentines for everybody in class, personally handed them out to everyone in envelopes with their name on them, instead of just having the teacher pass them out. I knew she was just equally nice to everyone, but I had that little ten-year-old's crush on her anyway.

"It was after I came back to school," she says, "when my mom and sister died. The teachers were really nice about everything. And my friends were nice, too, but I know that they always wanted me to go back to being Fun Cassie again."

"Yeah," I say. "And we would eat lunch in the music room."

I was just trying to be nice. Cassie told our teacher that she didn't want to go to the cafeteria, and I told Cassie that Mrs. Peters let me eat in the music room. She only joined me for a few weeks. It never occurred to me that Cassie even thought about it after she stopped——but I guess I didn't really give much thought to what was happening with her. I remember that she wasn't in school for a while, and then she was. I remember that there was something about a car accident. But it wasn't like we talked about our feelings much. Fourth grade was a tough year for me, too. That was when my dad lost his job, and things started getting scary at home. Mostly I just remember that, for a few weeks, instead of eating lunch by myself every day, the girl I liked best came into the music room and ate with me. I never thought about what it was like for her.

Cassie smiles. "You ate lunch with me every day,

and you never expected me to be a certain way. We would just sit there and eat, and then we'd play around on the piano a little."

And then she starts blushing, which is the least likely thing that has ever happened in the Texas State Capitol. If Zombie Sam Houston ambled through the doors and demanded to be governor again, it would be competing for second place.

"I mostly drew pictures of Batman," I say. "But you could play 'Moonlight Sonata.'"

Her smile widens. "I'm really glad you came," she says.

Man, so am I. Halfway through that year, when my dad finally left, we couldn't afford Catholic school tuition anymore. But now I wonder what would have happened if I'd stayed at St. Gabriel's. We both ended up at the same high school, but by that point, we were both sorted into our different groups—Cassie with the popular kids, me with the weirdos—and I can count on one hand the number of words we exchanged after St. Gabriel's, at least before today. But if things had been different? I might not have met Jesse and found my friends, which I always thought of as the one good thing that came out of my dad leaving. And then—well, shoot, I guess I'd be right where I am now, one of Cassie's friends, here at the Capitol with her.

"I'm glad I did, too," I say, and I mean it. It feels good to live up to who someone thinks I am, after all the ways I know I've let people down. Still, I'm not totally sure what it is I'm doing here, so I decide that, screw it, Cassie seems to think I'm okay, so I'll go ahead and ask her. "I have to admit, though, I haven't been following this super closely. What's all this about?" I wave my arms at the chaos that surrounds us, trying not to make eye contact with the guy who snapped at me when I got here. "Is this how this place usually is?"

Cassie laughs. "Oh my gosh, no. Not even a little bit. This is *bonkers*, Alex." I blush when she says my name. "It's *never* like this. But this is a super important bill. It'll end late-term abortions and make it so that abortion doctors have to be able to check their patients into the hospital. It could shrink the number of abortion clinics in Texas from, like, almost forty down to maybe five. They're saying five."

"Who's saying five?" I ask, because I don't know what else to say.

"*They* are," she whispers, gesturing with very small movements to the other people in line. She leans in conspiratorially. "The orangeshirts. Dewhurst has been pushing it——"

"Dewhurst?"

"He's the lieutenant governor, but everybody calls

him 'Mr. President' because he's the president of the Senate. He's in charge today," she says, then takes a sharp breath. "So many babies die in Texas, and this bill could really put a stop to so much of it."

"And everybody in orange is against the bill, and everybody in blue wants it?" I ask.

"Yeah," she says. "The orangeshirts started coming out last week—there was a hearing in one of the other buildings, and, like, hundreds of them showed up to testify. They were trying to run out the clock, basically."

"What do you mean, 'run out the clock'?"

"There are so many weird rules in politics!" She laughs. "Today is the last day of the legislative session, so the senators—the ones on our side, anyway —have to get this bill passed by midnight tonight, or it doesn't happen at all."

"So, like, the Texas legislature waited until the last day to do the assignment?" I ask. I've never related to my state senators more.

"Basically," she says. "But it shouldn't have taken this long, except that last week, the orangeshirts all showed up at once to testify about why they're for abortion, which would waste time and kill the bill. But it didn't work—one of our representatives on the committee figured out what they were doing, and he stopped the testimony."

"Wow," I say. I've never paid much attention to politics—I know my mom votes Republican, and I know Jesse's mom voted for Obama—but it sounds like some *Game of Thrones* business, like a scheme Tyrion would plan at the small council, until Littlefinger put a stop to it.

"I know, right?" Cassie leans close whenever she talks about the orangeshirts, like she doesn't want them to overhear. It's a thrill every time she does. She smells great, like just a tiny hint of honeysuckle and lavender. "So today is the last day of the session, which means that today is the last day that the bill can pass."

"So"—I lean in, and Cassie leans farther to meet me, and I breathe in how she smells and stare into her big brown eyes, which are so warm looking, and I try my very best not to let my train of thought derail—"the orangeshirts are trying to stop it?"

"Yep. The bill has to pass by midnight tonight, or it's over. And there's a Democrat, a state senator, who's supposed to start filibustering the bill," she explains. My face feels flush just being this close to her, and when she looks at me and starts laughing, I get even more embarrassed, like she's figured out that I'm crushing hard and she's about to sink my battleship. But she just says, "You know what a filibuster is, right?"

"I know that it is a word that I have heard before," I volunteer, relieved that she's assumed that my face is red because of my subpar understanding of state government and its various procedures.

"It's a thing you can do to block legislation, like a trick to get around the rules. The bill has to pass today, and a filibuster means—in Texas, anyway, it's different in Washington—that she is going to talk and talk all day so that nobody can vote on it. So this senator—Wendy Davis—is going to get up there and try to go and go and go to run out the clock. Until midnight."

"Holy shit," I say, then slap my hand over my mouth. Cassie doesn't seem like she swears much— she's definitely fond of "oh my gosh"—but she just smiles and gently puts her hand on my arm.

"Yeah," she says. "I know. They've got tricks they use to make it easier—she can basically get up there and read letters from people who are pro-abortion, or take questions from other senators, or whatever. But that's why it's so important that we're here. The more of us there are, the harder it'll be for her to look out and see all the people who are against what she's doing. Every blue shirt she sees is a reminder that there are babies on the line."

I nod, not wanting to point out that the blues are seriously outnumbered by the oranges here—and also not wanting to draw attention to the fact that my shirt is white.

She notices anyway.

"You should go see Father Mosier," she says, naming one of the priests at the church I play hooky from on Sundays. "He's downstairs somewhere, in one of the subbasements. He's got a whole box of those shirts." She gestures to the other side of the rotunda, where a family is lined up in blue T-shirts that read "Protect Texas Women" over a Texas flag.

"I'll go in a minute," I say. "I don't want to cut this line to get into . . . whatever it is you're waiting in line for."

"It's for the Senate gallery. This is where Wendy Davis has to do the filibuster. I want her to see me." There's a fierceness to Cassie when she says this. Then she shifts her stance and softens a little. "I don't think Wendy Davis is a bad person—I don't think *any* of the people in orange are bad people—but I don't think she's thought about this very much. At least, I don't think she's thought about it from the baby's perspective."

Man, everybody outside was busy shouting at each other that they were baby killers and murderers, or that they were stealing women's rights away. And here's Cassie, just super smart and nice about the whole thing, not calling anybody names. How often is the prettiest girl at school also the coolest?

And she thinks I'm a good person, which doesn't make a whole lot of sense to me, but maybe I was when we were in fourth grade. If this super-cool girl who's passionate about the things she cares about and determined to make a difference and do something good thinks I might be okay, then maybe I can be. Maybe I still have a shot at being the kind of person who Cassie Ramirez thought she was calling when she picked up her phone this morning.

One part of being that person sucks, though. When the line starts moving and the guy behind us looks at me, I wonder for a second if I could get away with just staying here and cutting the line. But I'm like thirty seconds into trying to be a better person today, so I take a step away.

"I should get to the back," I say. I peek inside the open doors to the gallery. It's a huge room—when I was walking up, I overheard someone say that it sat five hundred people—so maybe I'll still make it in?

I'm shocked to find that Cassie looks a little disappointed. "You're a good guy, Alex." Which, hell, I'm working on it. "I'll save you a seat for as long as they keep the doors open. You go downstairs and see Father Mosier and get yourself a blue shirt, and when you get in, we can hang out together. Cool?"

"Absolutely," I say. It sounds extremely cool to me.

* * *

EARLY FRESHMAN YEAR

It was the end of the second week of high school, and Jesse and I were on a mission. We rode our bikes after the last bell to Jerry's Artarama, the cool art supply store that didn't make you feel like you should be hanging out with the scrapbooking grandmas at Hobby Lobby. We locked our bikes up next to a couple of those really tall bikes that I'm not even sure how someone gets on. They probably belonged to art school college students with colorful hair and big mohawks who were there to buy paint and frames and, like, weird little knives for cutting single pieces of paper. We weren't really artists, but Jesse had spent the whole day working to convince me that we had a project to complete.

We stalked the aisles of Jerry's while the manager watched us closely to make sure we weren't graffiti kids there to shoplift spray paint. We weren't—we were there to get a collection of supplies that Jesse convinced me we needed: X-Acto knives, cardstock, vellum paper, tiny strands of hemp rope, lettering stamps, and super-intense liquid glue, all of which we paid for and stuffed into our backpacks for the ride back to his house.

When we got to Jesse's, we skipped the house and went around back to climb the stairs to the garage apartment that his mom let us hang out in. It was our retreat, and we'd spent hours out there, all by ourselves, ever since fifth grade. When we got to the door, there was a note from Bobby on it.

"GROUNDED FROM MY PHONE," it read. Bobby was a year older than us; he lived with his dad in the apartments a few blocks away, and we'd all become friends over the summer. His dad was a bully who pretended that it made him a stern disciplinarian instead of just an asshole. Even though Jesse's dad was dead and mine had pretty much disappeared into a bottle and taken off, we didn't envy Bobby's situation. "IF I CAN SNEAK OUT LATER I'LL BE BACK 2NITE."

Jesse stuffed the note in his back pocket, and we went inside, dumping our bounty of art supplies on the old thrift-store coffee table.

"Okay," he said. "I saw someone make one of these on YouTube. We have to get it just right."

When Jesse and I first started hanging out, we used to sit at the table and draw our own comic books, even though we swiped all the poses from comics we got from the library. We'd draw and talk about Batman or *Grand Theft Auto* or whatever funny things we'd seen on YouTube.

But by high school, the main topic of conversation was definitely girls. In middle school, we'd both been a pair of misfits, but over the past summer, Jesse got tall, his face cleared up, and girls suddenly wanted to talk to him. The only girl he wanted to talk to, though, was Shireen Dehghan, whose family moved to Austin from Dallas over the summer. Jesse had an idea: we were going to make mixtapes for our crushes, like they did in '90s movies. Except nobody had tape players, so we'd take these old cassettes his mom had, open them up, replace the tape inside with USB thumb drives with playlists on them, and glue the cassettes back together. That was what the X-Acto knives and glue were for. The cardstock, vellum paper, and hemp rope were for the sleeves, which would list the tracks on the playlists.

This was a great idea for Jesse, since Shireen was artsy and cool and seemed like the kind of person who'd be into a declaration of love with a soundtrack by all of Jesse's favorite bands. She and Jesse had been hanging out after school all week, and it seemed pretty clear that she liked him back.

"And you should make one, too. For Cassie Ramirez," Jesse had added when he told me about his plan that morning.

I'd spent the day rolling that possibility around in my mind and convincing myself I could do it. What kind of music did Cassie Ramirez listen to? I figured it was probably mostly Christian music, but I'd jotted down ideas in my notebook throughout the day. When I spotted her at lunch, sitting with her friends, I tried to imagine what it would be like to just walk over to her and hand her a cassette tape with a USB drive sticking out of it. We had barely exchanged two words since grade school. It seemed impossible. In my head, she was always "Cassie Ramirez," first and last name, and having a crush on her made about as much sense as having a crush on Taylor Swift.

"Okay," I said now, some of my ambivalence slipping into my voice, as I worked my X-Acto knife out of the package. "You really don't think it'd be weird as hell for me to give this tape to Cassie Ramirez?"

"Dude!" Jesse said. "You've had a crush on her since you were in Catholic school. You have to go for it."

"Maybe," I said. "But I don't think she's the same type of girl as Shireen. I think she's impressed by guys who, like, go build houses in Haiti over the summer."

"That would be a cool way to spend the summer," he said, wiggling his X-Acto knife in an attempt to pry a cassette casing apart.

"Let's see if we can figure out how to do a YouTube

arts and crafts project before we sign up to become carpenters," I told him as I poked around the side of my own cassette tape with my knife. I found a groove in the plastic and stuck the point in, then twisted it——and the case popped right apart.

"See? It's a sign," Jesse said. He jiggled his knife in his own tape and opened it up.

"Do you have your playlist all made?" I asked him. Even though I had pried apart his mom's old tape, it was getting harder and harder to imagine following through on this project. I was eager to change the subject to his plans for Shireen.

"I think so," he said. "I want her to think I'm cool, you know?" Jesse and I had only just started to know much of anything about music. So far, most of what we got came from Bobby, who was obsessed, curating epic playlists that we'd listen to all weekend long.

"What've you got?" I asked.

"I've got, like, new stuff and old stuff together, so she thinks I know a lot about music. I've got the National and Joy Division, St. Vincent and the Cure, and Band of Horses and Neil Young."

Shireen would love it. I tried to imagine playing St. Vincent or Joy Division for Cassie Ramirez, and the possibility of delivering the tape to her seemed even more distant.

"Do you want to put it on?" I asked.

He thought about it for a second. "Maybe? I want to know what you think . . ." Then he shook his head. "Nah. What if it's cheesy? It's better if I don't. But how about you? Why don't you put on your tape for Cassie Ramirez?"

I surprised myself by saying, "Okay, sure."

I had finished a pretty good rough sketch of the playlist in seventh period. I liked the idea of using somebody else's songs to tell a girl that I liked her; I was never great at using my own voice for stuff like that. But when I got up to plug my phone into the speakers, I knew that playing my Cassie Ramirez Playlist for Jesse was as close as I was ever going to get to giving it to her. Still, I wanted somebody to hear it. If I wasn't ready to tell Cassie Ramirez herself how I felt, I could at least show Jesse. I plugged the phone in, opened the app, and hit play.

The opening guitar melody of "Here Comes the Sun" started, and I blushed. I didn't know Cassie Ramirez at all, so most of the playlist was stuff like this—Beatles songs, Coldplay, Vampire Weekend, stuff that I was pretty sure she'd like because everybody liked it.

Jesse nodded. "Nice," he said. "Classic. Can't go wrong."

Despite his approval, I skipped past the song, and past "Fix You" and "Holiday." I quickly realized that I didn't even want Jesse to hear this playlist. As soon as the first few seconds of synths and bass from "Such Great Heights" by the Postal Service started, I reached to unplug my phone.

Jesse shot me a look. "Don't you dare!"

We stood there for a minute, listening to the singer go on about signs and freckles and mirror images, and then Jesse laughed, just a little.

"Oh, buddy," he said. "You got it *bad*, huh?"

I laughed. "There is no way on earth I am ever going to give this to her. You realize that, right?"

He nodded. I couldn't tell if he was disappointed or not, but he turned to me, seriously. "You're going to have to actually talk to her someday. You've got to promise me that you will."

10:55 am

I f Jesse were here, I imagine that he'd high-five me for the way waiting in line with Cassie went. But that's impossible, of course, so I decide to just do my best to keep it going. If a blue T-shirt is the price of admission to keep hanging out with Cassie Ramirez, I'll pay it.

The gallery is big, but there are a shitload of people here. Even with all those seats, as I walk past a zillion orangeshirts and a half-zillion blues, I can't imagine that I'm going to get in. I trot down the stairs and see people lined up all the way around the second-floor rotunda in a circle. I start counting people, lose track around two hundred, and remember that the gallery was already half full by the time Cassie got to the door. Welp.

If I'm not going to be sitting next to Cassie, I'm way less interested in finding Father Mosier and getting myself a blue T-shirt. But I promised her I would, and anyway, what's the alternative—I hop on my bike, ride home all sweaty again, then spend the next fourteen hours in front of my Xbox? That sounds even worse, so I begin my search for Father Mosier.

When you go to the Capitol on school field trips, you miss how big this place is. You see the rotunda, you see the Senate and House Chambers, someone points up and tells you that's where the offices are, and then you eat lunch in the cafeteria. You think you've pretty much seen it all. You spend most of the trip goofing off with your friends, or maybe trying to impress a girl or something, never thinking about all the people who work here. The fact that this is a place where actual government work goes down gets lost—it's just a fancy old building, built out of limestone (every tour guide gives you, like, a twenty-minute history of limestone), floors tiled with marble, and all of the doors dark, heavy wood. There are portraits of every governor of Texas, a truly stunning collection of dudes with goofy beards. But you never think about what they actually *do* here. What does lawmaking even look like?

Today, it looks like people sulking down the stairs after being rejected from the gallery. I can't get over the fact that so many hundreds—or is it thousands?—of people have decided to spend their day at the Capitol to watch some lady ramble on about abortion.

In addition to the upstairs floors, where the chambers and offices are, there are also downstairs floors. I hear the orangeshirts talk about going down there. I can't imagine what there is to do in a Capitol subbasement, but that's where Cassie said Father Mosier is.

I hang back from the orangeshirts and wait for the elevator next to a pair of blueshirts roughly my parents' age. I recognize the video camera guy with the goatee from before and his "cheerleaders of death" buddy—a couple of dudes you really want to party with on a Tuesday morning, let me tell you. The elevator makes a *ping* sound, and then the doors open. It's full, and everybody in it is wearing orange. They clear some space, but their faces go sour when they see the blue-shirted guys standing next to me. One of the orangeshirts grudgingly puts a hand to the elevator door to hold it open, but the guy with the goatee shakes his head.

"We'll catch the next one," he says.

I don't know these guys, though, and I don't really want the stink eye by association, so I slip into the elevator—

And get one of the nastiest looks I've ever been on the receiving end of.

From Shireen Dehghan.

I glare fire back at Shireen because I'll be damned

if she makes me feel like she belongs here and I don't—even if, you know, that's 100 percent true. She's wearing a dark orange shirt with the neck cut out. A picture of a flag with a uterus and the words "Come and Take It" is painted on the back, like the famous flag with the cannon that we learned about in Texas History. She's the second shortest person in the elevator, but only because one of the other people in here is an actual child. Shireen is still barely five feet tall. Her dark eyes glare at me from behind her short, curly, jet-black hair.

"What are *you* doing here?" she hisses at me. "Is this part of your community service or something?"

My heart beats fast just because I'm in the same place as Shireen. I have to will myself to come off as calm, like she's not getting to me. I just want this elevator ride to be over.

"I'm really interested in how government works," I say as slowly as I possibly can. "I find the journey of a bill as it becomes law to be a fascinating part of the civic process." The elevator dings, and the door opens on the first subbasement. Wendy Davis isn't the only one who can run out the clock talking nonsense. If I'm even a little bit lucky, those will be the last words I ever exchange with Shireen.

Shireen moves quickly to get out of the elevator, which is great—she hates this as much as I do. I decide to get off at the next floor, to minimize the chance that I ever have to see her again.

On the lower level, the blueshirt goatee guy and his buddy catch up to me. They keep getting dirty looks from everybody in orange, so I start walking really slowly, to make it look less like I'm the third member of their group and more like I just, oops, got off the elevator at the same time. I measure my steps carefully—a skill I developed to evade hallway bullies at school—and keep my eyes fixed directly ahead of me, at some nonexistent point out in the distance. In some ways, being at the Capitol today feels a lot like being in school, even if that may just be because I'm trying to avoid Shireen again.

What the hell is she doing here? Then I realize, duh, of course she's here. She always was the most political one of us. She got us to all go door-knocking for Obama last year (Jesse's mom loved her). She brought petitions to school and got us all to sign them. In fact, if things had played out differently over the past year, I might have come here with her and Jesse and the rest of our friends.

But I'm here with Cassie, and I promised her I'd get a shirt from Father Mosier. I see a bunch of blueshirts in the same T-shirt I'm supposed to acquire standing at the end of the hall, near doors that lead outside. I walk over and see Father Mosier's heavyset frame, thinning hair, and mustache. He's standing near a box of T-shirts. He's surrounded by people I recognize from church, all holding placards and signs.

As I step toward them, I hear chanting—"Life—yes! Abortion—no!"—and, gun-shy from being glared at when I was with the blueshirts by the elevator, sidestep the group, even though everyone seems really friendly and happy to see me. I notice Mrs. Lesner, my second-grade teacher, and she lets a big smile break out on her round face.

"God bless you, Alex," she says, and I return her smile.

"Do you need a T-shirt?" Father Mosier asks me, and I nod. He sizes me up with a glance. "Large?"

"Medium," I say, and he digs around in the box.

He hands me the shirt but is slow to relinquish it when I reach for it. "You know," he says, "I haven't seen you around on Sundays lately."

I give a vague half smile and a shrug. "I've been there," I lie, which I guess means I'm *really* not much of a Catholic, because I don't even feel bad for lying to a priest.

He smiles. "Good man," he says as he hands over the shirt. "Stay awhile and pray with us?"

"Definitely," I say. Another lie! "I'm going to go in and look for Cassie first, though, and then we'll both come out."

"Cassie Ramirez?" Father Mosier asks with what sounds like disbelief, like *what is Cassie Ramirez doing hanging out with you.* "She's a good egg."

"Yes, sir," I say, because I don't know what else to say. Father Mosier seems like a nice enough man, but I don't know him well. This is probably the most I've ever talked to the guy. That includes confession, where I would usually just recite the basics ("I lied to my parents, I stayed out past curfew with my friends, I took the Lord's name in vain," leaving out how many goddamn times I did it), and he'd hit me back with a rote atonement—a half-dozen Hail Marys and an Our Father or two.

I'm turning to walk away when I feel my phone buzz in my pocket. It's Cassie.

Had to give up yr seat :(The action is officially underway though! I'll text you around lunchtime?

Lunch with Cassie! My heart picks up. I put the T-shirt on to snap a selfie and send the photo back to her. *Found Father Mosier! See you in a bit,* I send.

I start walking back down the hallway and spot a couple of girls not much older than me chatting. One of them has blond hair and a really pretty smile that she flashes as she talks with her friend, but when I walk past, they both look at me like I'm made out of cancer. They are, of course, both wearing orange.

So that's what it's like to take a side.

They're not the only ones looking, either. I usually feel like I'm 90 percent invisible in any room, which I don't always love, but I sure miss it right now. Everybody in the hallway near me is wearing orange and glaring like I'm a member of a warring House in Westeros.

It's not like I believe any of these people would be my friend if I were wearing a different color T-shirt, but I hate feeling this exposed. Being invisible beats the hell out of being the enemy, and I don't even know why I'm wearing this T-shirt if I'm not sitting next to Cassie to support her.

Sorry, Father Mosier, I think to myself as I duck down a side hallway that seems empty. I guess I'll tell him about it in confession if I ever go back to church. As soon as he and Mrs. Lesner can't see me, I pull the blue shirt over my head and stuff it into my bag.

Walking back out into the hallway, it's like resetting a video game. Thirty seconds ago, these people hated me, but now they don't even notice me. I don't think anybody saw my face at all, just the color of my T-shirt. I don't know what that says about politics, but I don't really care—I'm just glad to be invisible.

I walk back up one flight of stairs to the first subbasement. The halls are a lot less crowded than on the lower level. Outside one of the big rooms, though, there are a few people milling around. The door to the room is wide open, and I peek inside. The room has a large, movie theater–style screen, and it's playing what looks like a live feed from the Senate floor.

"What's going on in there?" I ask a college-aged guy in orange who probably would have hated me if he had seen me two minutes ago.

"It's the overflow room," he says, "to watch the filibuster."

Most of the people in the room are wearing orange, and they're rowdy as they watch the livestream. On the screen, a man in a suit is talking on the floor of the Senate. He looks young, at least for a politician, and he's explaining the purpose of the bill. It's going to ban abortion at twenty weeks (boos!); "raise all clinics to the ambulatory surgical center standard," whatever that means (more boos!); and require doctors to have admitting privileges at hospitals (which sounds like it should be a good thing for doctors to have? But somehow, even boos for that!). Then he's interrupted by an older man in a stiff-looking suit at the head of the chamber, whose name flashes on the screen—Lt. Governor David Dewhurst.

"I wonder if I could interrupt you just for a moment," Lieutenant Governor Dewhurst says. "Senator Davis, yesterday you gave me a sheet indicating it was your intention to filibuster?"

A different speaker answers the question this time——a petite blond woman. *So that's Wendy Davis,* I think. She reminds me of my mom——her hair's longer, and she's a little more stylish, but they both have the same taste in hot-pink running shoes.

"Yes, Mr. President," Wendy Davis says, "I intended to speak for an extended period of time on the bill. Thank you very much."

11:18 am

Before Wendy Davis starts speaking, David Dewhurst interrupts her—something about a Senator Van de Putte, who's asked to be excused—and the room hisses. It's very orange in here, and these people do not seem to like David Dewhurst one bit.

Then it's Wendy Davis's turn, and the room falls silent. What she's saying is boring—something about "how we wound up at this moment, on this day, on the Senate floor, debating this bill"—and it's like everything she says, she finds five words to say it when one would do. Which, I guess, *is* what she's doing, since she has to stretch all of this out for thirteen hours. But even so, I hear a woman in orange say to her little girl that "this is history right here," and maybe she's right? So I make myself pay attention.

The senator's talking about the same stuff Cassie told me about this morning, but she makes it all sound shocking and wrong. When Cassie explained how the bill would stop late-term abortions, require doctors to be able to check patients into the hospital, and raise clinic standards, those all sounded like good things. But when Wendy Davis talks about how she's going to speak today for the voices that didn't get heard, that sounds like a good thing, too. I sit and listen for a few minutes as she talks dramatically about "the dark place" the bill will take us, and how it hurts women and families. But I don't understand how that could be true.

Everybody else in the room is watching the screen like it's the opening kickoff of the Super Bowl or the part at the end of a Marvel movie where Samuel L. Jackson is gonna show up, but the disconnect between how the senator talks about this and how Cassie talked about it earlier just makes me hate politics. Maybe what Wendy Davis is saying is right, but how is anybody supposed to know that, when she talks about the other side like they're history's greatest monsters? I don't know how it could be bad for women if clinics are better, or if their doctors can take them to the hospital, but when Wendy Davis talks about those things, she says they're examples of "blind partisanship" and "personal political am-bition," without explaining why. I stand up to leave the room.

I decide to go upstairs and get in line for the gallery, so I can wait for a chance to hang out with

Cassie, when I hear a familiar voice from outside the room.

"They said we can set up in room E2.002. Can you tweet that?"

I recognize Debbie Monaghan's voice. She's Mr. Monaghan's daughter, and she and my mom have been friends through church for as long as I can remember. They both sing in the choir, and she was my confirmation sponsor.

When I step out of the auditorium and into the hallway, I see her: tall stature, long brown hair, glasses that are always at the tip of her nose, and—to my shock—an orange "Stand with Texas Women" T-shirt.

"Ms. Monaghan?" I say as I approach.

"Alex? For the love of god, call me Debbie, will you? I feel old enough here right now." She nods at a girl about my age in an orange shirt, who's frantically typing away on her phone.

"Sorry, Debbie," I mumble.

"What are you doing here?" she asks, then laughs. "Whatever—I'm glad you're here. Thank goodness you're not one of those blueshirt kids running around with tape on your mouth. You mind helping out?"

"Sure," I say, because I don't know how *not* to say "sure" when someone like Debbie Monaghan asks me for help. "What can I do?"

"We'll be setting up food and coffee and stuff in the lower-level basement. Room E2.002. Can you go down there and get started on that? Just take the tables out of whatever other rooms are unlocked."

The idea of walking around the Texas State Capitol subbasement to peek into conference rooms and steal the tables doesn't exactly thrill me, but I'm not going to say that to Debbie Monaghan, whose voice drops two octaves and whose sentences get very crisp when she shifts into "take charge of things" mode.

"Yeah," I say. "Okay. You want me to do that by myself?"

Debbie turns to the girl she'd previously instructed to tweet. "What are you doing?" she asks.

"I was about to live-tweet the filibuster," the girl says.

"Right, okay—do that, but stay around here, will you? I might need your Twitter again," Debbie barks.

The girl steps into the auditorium, and Debbie turns to me, pausing to breathe for the first time since I saw her.

"That girl—Vickie—she's younger than you are, but she has fifteen thousand followers on Twitter. She takes these little six-second videos of her cat that people love. She sends a message, and it goes everywhere. That's how we're feeding so many people—Vickie and the other people here who have big Twitter accounts, they're soliciting donations. We got seventy-five pizzas from people all over the world on Sunday," she says. "I bet today will be even bigger."

"From all over the world?" I'm suddenly picturing a tiny army of pizza delivery drones being sent all the way from Tokyo, stopping in Ireland to pick up more, and detouring to Canada to add to their stack before heading down to the Capitol in Austin for some reason. "People really care that much about what's happening here?"

"It starts here, it goes other places eventually," she says. "This bill is some serious bullshit, Alex. Right now, they don't worry about these things in places like New York and California—but it's coming for them, too. These fucking bills target perfectly good and legal clinics by passing restrictions that are impossible for them to meet. They get to claim it's all in the name of 'women's health,' while women are out there suffering because the bills managed to close every clinic within five hours of them."

Did my confirmation sponsor just say the words *fuck* and *bullshit*? I guess she's Mr. Monaghan's daughter, but still. I'm seeing a whole new side to this woman who wears puff-painted sweatshirts in the winter and who has a cat named Lady Superstar.

"Isn't that a good thing, though?" I ask, then

immediately get self-conscious. "I mean, I know you're Catholic."

To my relief, Debbie doesn't start swearing at me. Instead, she laughs. "God gave everybody free will, Alex, and He lets us use it to do what we will with our lives. Sounds pretty pro-choice to me."

"Man, tell that to Father Mosier out there," I say.

Debbie reaches into her big canvas tote bag, retrieves a rolled-up orange sign, and shows it to me. Its big white cut-out lettering reads "God Is Pro-Choice," with big smiley faces in the Os. "Believe me," she says. "I have."

I smile at her sign. I don't know if I believe in God, but when she says that he is pro-choice, that makes sense to me, too.

"Anyway," she says, "can you go downstairs and get set up? I've got more volunteers to coordinate up here——there's so much organizing to do with everybody, it's like herding cats."

Yikes. But if Debbie Monaghan trusts me to do something, I'll find a way to get it done. I nod, then walk over to the elevator and push the button. A moment later, the door opens, a smattering of orangeshirts get out, and I step in to go downstairs.

In the lower subbasement, I walk along the hallway, looking for signs indicating which room might be E2.002. My phone buzzes again. It's Cassie.

This is sooooo boring, her text reads.

I text back, *maybe she'll start singing?*

only 12 hours to go.

I guess that means Cassie's not optimistic that Wendy Davis will call it an early day.

i bet she won't make it that long, I text, and she sends me back a smiley face.

I check out the sign-plate near the door to a big room—E2.002, mission accomplished! I turn around to figure out where to get the tables from, and I see a couple of guys who look like they're probably in college behind me. They're wearing orange and opening the doors to a room across the hall.

"Did Debbie send you?" I ask them.

"I'm not sure what her name is," one of the guys says.

"Tall lady, barks orders?" I ask.

"Yeah."

"Me too," I say. "My name's Alex."

"Cool, man," he says, and then he goes into the room across the hall. He turns to his buddy and says, "I say, we must get the tables and chairs now!" in a fake British accent; the other guy barks, "Right, quite right," and they both laugh at whatever bit they're doing and start raiding the room for stuff to put food on. I just follow along and pick up chairs while they ignore me.

Hanging out with random guys I don't know who don't care if I get their jokes is something I'm trying to do a whole lot less of. In fact, avoiding situations where I'm following some dudes around and doing whatever they're doing is kind of one of the terms of my deferred prosecution deal. All I know is this isn't much fun, and texting with Cassie in the hope that maybe I'll get to go into the gallery to hang out with her for a while is starting to make me feel like a sucker. As the orange bros wander by the other rooms, I remind myself that I'm not here to hang out with them. I'm here because I don't know how to say no to Debbie Monaghan.

Speaking of things that suck, Room E2.002 isn't so hot, either. It's got blueish-green carpet and fluorescent lights in the ceiling, and it looks a lot like the band room at school. All the furniture, which is just some cheap chairs and tables, looks like it came from a closeout deal at an office supply store.

"Get more tables," one of the orange dudes says to the other. "Remember how many pizzas there were on Sunday?" And the other one says, "Quite right," in that fake accent again.

While they reminisce over the number of pizzas they saw on Sunday, I arrange the other tables in a pattern designed to approximate the layout of a restaurant, then place the chairs around them. There you go, Debbie——and you're welcome, pro-choice pro-testers, for your comfortable table setting at which you will eat your one thousand free pizzas that were sent by people from Guam or wherever.

The orange dudes, satisfied with the job, head toward the elevator, and I follow, keeping my distance so I don't have to feel like a tagalong. Maybe it's that they remind me of people I'd rather forget, but my enthusiasm for hanging out at the Capitol today is just about running out. The orangeshirt guys seem like jerks. The blueshirt guys with the video camera and goatees seem like jerks. Shireen Dehghan is running around here somewhere. Father Mosier and my second-grade teacher are here, and they're going to look at me like I'm a big disappointment if I'm not wearing a blue T-shirt when they see me——but if I *do* wear a blue T-shirt, most of the people walking around are going to look at me like I showed up at Coachella with a floating arrow over my head with the words "This Guy Is a Cop" written on it. And I can't even get into the room where Cassie is, which is my main reason for being here.

I skip the elevator and take the stairs up to the first basement level, mostly just to slow down and delay having to figure out what I'm going to do next. If I leave, the idea of hanging out with Cassie and getting to know her better is going to fart away, but just sticking around here aimlessly, pausing occasionally to watch a state senator talk about literally nothing on a big TV, is pretty pathetic.

When I get to the next level, Debbie Monaghan is pacing by the stairs and pulling on a strand of her hair like she wants to rip it off. She's grumbling something on the phone and pressing her lips together like she's trying not to scream. I try to walk past her without her noticing, but she waves me over. Please tell me she doesn't need me to move more furniture.

"Okay," she says. "Okay, I understand. I'll figure something out."

She ends the call, and I try to look like I'm not dreading whatever she's about to ask me to do.

"Hey," she says. "I need you to do me a favor."

"What's going on?" I ask, mentally running through a list of excuses for why I can't help. Unfortunately, she knows exactly how not-busy I am this summer.

"It's my dad," she says, shaking her head. "He's being difficult. He hates the center anyway, and now he's saying that one of the employees was being condescending, so he got indignant."

Well, that changes things. I picture Mr. Monaghan letting some stunned-looking employee know that his eyes might be going, but his ears and brain work just fine, and he's not gonna take any more of this crap.

"'I fought in the war; you treat me with some respect!'" I say.

"Yeah, with a couple more f-bombs in there," she says. "Anyway, he can't stay there today, and I have to stick around here. There's a ton to coordinate. Can you go pick him up? He likes you a lot."

"I'd be happy to." It's actually true, so I'm not even feeding her an excuse when I add, "But he'd have to ride on my handlebars."

"Oh, shit," she says. "That's right." She sighs, then reaches into her purse for her keys. "You can take my car. Do you—hell—can you drive a stick?"

I shake my head. I can barely drive an automatic. School, Jesse's house, work (when I had a job), the Austin Adult Day Care Center, and anywhere else I would go is within biking distance of my house, so I haven't bothered to spend much time behind the wheel. Somehow having an *actual* reason for why I can't help with this favor makes me feel crappier than making up a reason why I wouldn't be able to make 700 gallons of coffee or whatever for her orange friends to drink.

"Okay. Okay, shit. Knew it was too good to be true that you'd be here." She shakes her head and purses her lips, frustrated. I want to offer some sort of suggestion to help, but I've got nothing.

Out of the corner of my eye, I spot a girl with

short black hair and olive skin in the auditorium where a screen shows Wendy Davis reading a letter from the American College of Obstetricians and Gynecologists, who apparently aren't psyched about this bill, either. The girl is wearing an orange shirt, obviously, with the neck cut out.

Debbie follows my gaze and stage-whispers, "Shireen!"

I get that tingling sensation behind my ears that you get when you realize you left the folder with your homework in it on the counter this morning.

Sure enough, Shireen Dehghan turns toward us.

She takes a step in our direction. When she sees me, she makes the same face you'd make if you walked past a Taco Cabana dumpster on a hot day.

"What's up?" she asks Debbie.

"I need you to do me a favor. Do you have your car here?"

Shireen nods cautiously, eyeing me the same way all the orangeshirts did when I was wearing blue. I notice that I've been grinding my teeth for the past twenty seconds.

"Great," Debbie says, oblivious. "I need you to take Alex here to the adult day care center on 38th Street—Alex knows where it is—and go pick up my dad. Just bring him back here."

"You can just tell me how to get there and I can

go get him by myself," Shireen offers, which sounds like a great idea to me, too.

"No, Alex knows him. He's in a mood. He's not going to get into a car with a stranger." Debbie shakes her head.

"And Alex can't go by himself because he's on a bike?" Shireen says it like I'm the saddest loser in the history of sad losers.

Debbie throws up her hands, looking at me and Shireen like we're both being idiots, even though I haven't done anything but stand here and set my lower jaw like I might need it to chew through some ropes at some point. "For fuck's sake, kids. Can you just please go help me out? I promised Brittany from Planned Parenthood I would be at the Capitol all day, and there's a ton to do here."

I nod and decide to speak for both of us, because if *Shireen's* the one who says it first, I'll probably end up declaring that now is a perfect time for me to learn to drive a stick shift, just so I don't have to agree with her.

"We'll go get him," I say.

Shireen wrinkles her nose, making a face like she just caught somebody peeing on the sidewalk in broad daylight.

"Great," Debbie says. "Terrific. *Thank you.*" She stresses it hard, like she's being sarcastic and not actually grateful to us for agreeing to the sacrifice of enduring an hour in one another's company.

Before we go, she reaches into her backpack and produces two orange T-shirts, which she hands to me.

"Here you go. One for Dad, one for you. Thanks," she says, this time like she means it. "I appreciate it."

I take the "Stand with Texas Women" T-shirts and stuff them in my bag, right next to the blue shirt I got from Father Mosier that says "Protect Texas Women." So this is politics: T-shirts. I think of Cassie in her blue dress, and I smile, a big screw-all-of-this smile that must piss Shireen off, because she turns wordlessly and starts making long strides toward the elevators.

When Shireen pushes the button and it doesn't immediately light up, she steps toward the stairs and takes them two at a time. I'd be the one walking fast like I'm trying to get away from her, except I don't know where the car is parked. Either way, though, I'm very much in favor of this "let's not say a word to each other" policy that Shireen has instituted for our mission. We power through the rotunda, which has no line in it now——just groups of people, some of them in orange with signs, some of them in blue in a prayer circle——and stride out the south exit of the Capitol toward Shireen's little silver Honda Civic, where I used to spend a lot of time, and which fills me with a deep sense of shame when I actually see it.

It's been more than six months since the last time I was in Shireen's car, but I know the Civic well. I've gotten rides home from school in it. I've driven through the Taco Cabana drive-thru in the middle of the night in it. I've sat in the back seat next to Shireen's friend Holly. I'm pretty sure Shireen and Jesse hoped that if Shireen took a turn real sharp, and it made our bodies smoosh together somehow, it would lead to the two of us making out—even though Holly and I had both thought about whether we were interested and settled on "nah."

Walking to the Civic now, though, is really different. For one, it's just the two of us, which isn't how things with me and Shireen usually were. We hung out with the same people, a lot, over a long stretch of time. We worked on projects together when I was still doing theater, and we sat near each other in classes when we were the only people from our group there. But the number of times that Shireen and I were the only two people in a room could fit on one hand, and most of those times, we were probably just waiting for Jesse or Holly or Bobby to get back from the bathroom.

The other reason it feels different is because the car *looks* different now. The little Civic always had a lot of personality—it had faded paint and a million stickers and a little Hula Girl on the dashboard, and Bobby used to write messages in the back window with his finger, which annoyed the hell out of Shireen—but now, as we near the parking spot south of the Capitol on Congress Avenue, it's just a car. The paint job is fresh, the stickers are gone, the windows are tinted, and through the tint, by the driver's side, there's the blinking light of an expensive new car alarm.

Shireen's silent as she unlocks the car, and I feel so weird as I get in that I return the favor and ignore her, too.

She starts the car, and alas, the stereo starts playing *Coexist* by the xx. It's an album I've listened to a lot—in this car, in the garage apartment behind Jesse's house, and on my headphones late at night by myself. But not in the past six months.

I glare at Shireen, like she chose this music on purpose to annoy me, even though there's no way that when she drove downtown this morning she could have guessed that I'd end up sitting in her passenger seat. It's not like she knows that I've been avoiding this album, and the ones by the Antlers and the National and Sharon Van Etten, that make me feel like I'm still in the garage apartment with a group of friends, instead of spending my summer reading a zillion-page fantasy epic to an old man who, apparently, gets too cranky sometimes to stay at the adult day care center his daughter pays for.

I don't want to think about any of that right now, but then the fucking singer starts singing about a life left behind. I'm about to dive into a deep pool of self-pity when Shireen finally turns the music down and looks at me.

"So what are you doing at the Capitol in the first place? I didn't see you here any of the other days," she says, and it's not exactly a question.

"I wasn't here the other days. I don't really know why I'm here today," I admit, finally, which feels kind of good. "I'm here because Cassie asked me to go."

"Cassie? Cassie Ramirez?" She snorts. "You're hanging out with Cassie Ramirez these days? Okay, dude."

"What's wrong with Cassie Ramirez?" I didn't know they knew each other.

"Oh, nothing," she snaps. "She's just so . . . *nice.*"

"Why are *you* here?" I ask her.

"Because it's fucking important," she says. "Jesus Christ, dude. They're going to basically make abortion illegal in Texas, and they're lying about what they're doing and why. And they're sneaking all this shit in during the summer like nobody is even looking. Well, I'm fucking looking."

She gets that monologue out, then pauses for a moment and looks at me again. "Wait a second. If you're here with Cassie——you're not on our side, are you? You're one of the blueshirts."

I sit silently for a moment. I don't like Shireen, but I like being thrown into a category like that even less.

"I'm a whiteshirt," I say finally.

Shireen snorts again, like this isn't much of an answer. But she doesn't say anything, just turns the music back up, louder this time, and it all makes me feel guilty and as shallow and small as the last time I saw her and Jesse.

* * *

FALL OF JUNIOR YEAR

The first time Shireen showed up at the garage apartment with a 24-pack of Lone Star tall boys and a bag of weed, I didn't make a big deal of it. She and Holly, whose older sister bought it for them, were psyched, though.

"Check out what *we* got," Holly said to nobody in particular when they came in.

I didn't feel great about it——the smell of beer always made me think of my dad, and not in good ways——but I also didn't want to be a buzzkill, so I just passed when Jesse offered me one. It was his birthday. Our friend group at school had grown since he and Shireen had consolidated power as the king and queen of the weirdos, so there were a bunch of people over. As the night went on, I scooted back from the circle when they passed the bowl around, and Jesse and Bobby spoke up for me—"Nah, Alex isn't into that"—which kept me from feeling too out of place. I decided to make myself part of the night by playing DJ on my phone. *Coexist* had just come out, so I put that on, and everybody seemed to enjoy the low-key vibe. I did, too. But the party that started on Jesse's birthday only ramped up as we got further into the school year.

One night after work, I got a ride to Jesse's house from Tommy Richman, Jacob Kohler's best friend and one of the delivery drivers at Double Dave's. Tommy was usually a jerk when he and Jacob were together, but by himself, he was all right.

"Huh, this is where that dude lives?" he said when we pulled up. "Cool house."

I got out and headed to the garage apartment. We'd had a couple of leftover pizzas at work, so I'd boxed them up, figuring they'd make me popular when I got inside. It was a little after midnight, but things were still going strong. This was how it usually was on the weekends—it turned out, if you have a place where everybody can chill all weekend long and the only adult supervision is in another building, it makes your place the popular hangout.

I scanned the room and mostly saw people I knew. There were Jesse and Bobby; Shireen and Holly, who must have played the "let's tell our parents that we're spending the night at each other's house" game; a couple of guys I knew from school who Jesse and I had always been friendly with; three girls from Round Rock who Holly was friends with, and some dude they brought with them; and then a handful of people that Bobby knew. They were a little older. One of the girls was kind of cute.

Most everybody was sitting either on the floor or on the cheap couches we'd picked up from Goodwill over the summer. I put the pizzas down on the coffee table in the center, and people immediately lunged for them.

"Oh, hell yeah!" Bobby said. "Alex the Hero."

Jesse was flipping through horror movies on Netflix. "Should we do *Paranormal Activity* or *Insidious*?"

Shireen cast a vote for *Paranormal Activity 3*, which was my favorite, so I shouted a second.

"*Paranormal 3* going once, twice, sold," Jesse said, like an auctioneer.

The movie started, and I settled in. This had become my standard way of doing nights at

Jesse's——staying sober while everyone else was buzzed or stoned. I might have missed the old days when it didn't smell like beer and weed all the time, but at least we could all still hang out and watch a movie. We turned down the lights and cracked each other up with punchlines as we watched the two little girls get haunted to all hell.

The dude from Round Rock nodded his head toward the pizzas and looked at me. "Hey, are those yours? Trade you a beer for a slice."

"All yours," I said. He tried to hand me a can of Lone Star, but I shook my head. "I'm good."

"Really? Sweet," he said.

I turned my attention back to the movie, wondering if there were any sodas in the fridge but not wanting to lose my seat. After a minute, the door opened, and four guys I didn't know came in. They looked older, like they were in college, which some of Bobby's friends were. Bobby hopped up.

"Bro!" he said. "You got the goodies?"

One guy nodded and pulled out a bag of pills. "Want to smoke a bowl and pre-game?"

Everybody turned to form a circle, which pretty much killed the movie-watching part of the evening. Bobby packed a bowl, and I scooted back a few inches to try to get out of the circle. The guy who brought the bag took a hit when it was his turn, then passed the bowl to me.

"No, thanks," I said. He shrugged and passed it over me to Holly. I felt a little bit like my vegetarian cousin who ate a bowl of cornflakes on Thanksgiving.

Sometimes the conversation as people got high was interesting—like, creative stoner philosophy stuff— but tonight, it was mostly about how strong the weed was. After a minute of talk about how somebody's friend's cousin or whatever had a hookup for the good stuff, the bowl came back my way again.

"I'm good," I said to the same guy who'd offered it to me last time.

"I'm good," he said back, then passed it over to Holly.

I figured this was going to be a boring night, so I went into Jesse's room to look for his iPad so I could play *Bejeweled*—but the cute girl from Round Rock was in there with one of Bobby's friends, so I popped back out.

Another one of the older dudes was in the kitchen, stabbing a beer can with a knife and holding it sideways. "Dude," he said. "Ten bucks says I can shotgun one of these faster than you can."

I shook my head and looked over to the circle, where Bobby was repacking the bowl. It all started to feel like too much, so I went into the bathroom and sat on the edge of the tub.

I had spent a fair bit of time hiding in the bathroom when I was a kid, trying to get away from my dad. Seeing all the Lone Star cans around the garage apartment made me feel like I was ten years old again. I hated it—this place had always felt like my safe haven, and now I was hiding in the bathroom again.

Before I could get too into my feelings about it, the dude from Round Rock who'd offered to trade me a beer burst in, pushed past me to the toilet, and immediately started puking. Outside the bathroom, everybody was laughing.

I stepped out, and everybody started laughing even harder. "Oh shit," Bobby said. "Did that dude, like, puke on your dick?"

I just shook my head and tried to figure out what I was supposed to do with myself. I pulled out my phone, but the battery was at like 4 percent. I guess my new activity would be charging my phone? But then that older dude who kept trying to pass me weed came over and put his arm around me, leading me back to the circle where everybody seemed pretty wasted.

"Hey, man," he said. "I got you. You want one of these?" He could barely suppress a laugh as he rubbed a couple of small, round, greenish-gray pills between his fingers.

"No, thanks," I said.

"No, thanks!" he said back, in a high-pitched voice, like I was a gigantic uncool baby.

I looked over to Jesse for some help. He was sitting on a couch cushion, his cigarette burning down toward his fingers, seeming pretty out of it.

"No, thanks," he said to no one in particular. Then he giggled and put his head on Shireen's shoulder. I didn't know if he was making fun of me or just repeating the last thing he heard. I didn't know if he knew, either. All I knew was that I couldn't count on him anymore.

I dipped my head to get away from the guy with the pills, went into the kitchen, and opened the fridge just to give myself something to do.

"If you're getting a beer, bro, bring me one, too?" the dude yelled.

I kept my face in the fridge and ran through my options. I didn't have my bike. It was late. If I called my mom, I'd have to tell her something about what happened, and that would mean the end of hanging out at Jesse's, at a minimum. I wasn't ready to admit to myself that there wasn't much there for me anyway.

I could have gone to the main house to wake up Jesse's mom and ask for a ride home, made up some sort of emergency that didn't implicate anybody else, but that would have been even worse. I wasn't going to snitch about what was going on back here, so I'd have to pretend to her that everything was normal. She let us get away with so much because she felt guilty that she was so busy being a college professor while Jesse was growing up without a dad, and she said yes to pretty much everything he ever asked for. That had been awesome when it meant ordering us Chinese food for delivery while we stayed up all night playing video games, but it had clearly passed a tipping point.

I'd exhausted the amount of time a person could reasonably spend with his face inside of a refrigerator, so I grabbed a Mountain Dew and shut the door. The party seemed like it was losing some steam. I grabbed a pillow off the back of the couch and lay down on the floor of the kitchen to sleep. I woke up a few hours later, just as the sun started to crash through the window. I stepped over some sleeping people I didn't even know, grabbed my backpack, and looked over to Jesse's bed. He and Shireen were asleep, and I felt like garbage. I thought back to Jesse's birthday over the summer, when she'd brought the beer and weed over for the first time, and I knew whose fault it was that everything was like this now.

I tiptoed past these people whose faces I didn't

recognize, whose names I didn't know, who were all asleep in this place where I had been hanging out since I was in fifth grade, and thought about how I used to have a best friend who didn't make me feel like an out-of-place loser. I grabbed my shoes, carried them outside, and laced them onto my feet on the stairs. I walked along the driveway, passing Shireen's silver Honda Civic, and began the long trek home.

* * *

I'm only yanked out of this whole bummed-out train of thought that accompanies the xx record because Shireen slams on the brakes—she must have done that deliberately—and parks at the adult day care center.

"So this is where Debbie's dad is?" she says, still not really a question.

"Yeah, Mr. Monaghan. Do you want to come in, or wait here?" I ask.

Shireen shrugs. "I don't know, dude. I don't know this guy, but he sounds like a handful. Do you need me to help, or will I just stress him out?"

"He's not a handful," I snap, filled with righteous anger, which is all the more satisfying because it's directed at Shireen. "He just doesn't like to take any shit from people."

Shireen nods, not particularly interested. "All right. You go get him, I guess. I'll wait here."

I walk quickly into the center, retracing my steps from—was it really only three hours ago? When I enter the room with the armchairs and the piano, Mr. Monaghan is sitting in a small wooden kitchen chair, visibly seething, while a guy in his thirties wearing scrubs stands just outside of swinging distance from him.

"Mr. Monaghan?" I say, walking over. He looks in my direction, and I remember that he can't see me very well and isn't expecting me. "It's Alex."

"Alex?" he says. "What the hell are you doing here? Where's Debbie?"

"She's busy at the Capitol," I tell him. "She sent me."

"Am I gonna ride out of here on your bike or what?"

"No, I'm with—" I'm not about to call Shireen a friend. "Someone else is here to drive."

His eyes narrow. He throws a glare at the guy in the scrubs, then shakes his head. "Fine," he says, finally.

"Do you have everything you need?" I ask.

"Everything except my fucking dignity," he says, again casting his gaze toward the guy in scrubs, who stares intently at the wall just past Mr. Monaghan's shoulder.

I hold out my arms like *what do you want me to do*, and he finally rises from his chair. I step toward him, in case he needs help walking or anything, but he's fine—all things told, he's pretty spry for eighty-five.

He walks in front of me to get out the door, like he can't wait to get the hell out of the adult day care center. I follow right behind him, then step in front when we get to the sidewalk, so I can direct him to Shireen's car. I open the back door for him, and he shakes off my silent offer of assistance.

When we're all in the car, he ignores Shireen in favor of asking the more burning question: "So where are you taking me?"

"To the Capitol," I say. I reach into my bag and toss him his orange shirt. "Debbie thought it was important that you put this on."

"Oh, Jesus," he says. "Fucking politics." But he removes his outermost flannel shirt and puts the orange tee on. It's not exactly stylish, but it looks better than his previous combination, though that's not saying much.

"I'm Shireen, by the way," Shireen says after he's settled.

I was enjoying watching him ignore her, but now he becomes downright gentlemanly.

"How do you do, miss," he says. "My name's Sean, but this guy"—he kicks my seat—"insists on calling me 'Mr. Monaghan' like I'm an old man or something."

"He's cruel like that," she says, and for some reason it actually hurts my feelings. I don't like the idea of Shireen and Mr. Monaghan making jokes about me.

"Sorry, *Sean*," I say. "I'll try to remind you that you're only as old as you feel."

Mr. Monaghan laughs. "You're in a mood, kid," he says. "How are things down there, anyway? Is she giving those fuckers the what-for?"

I can only assume that "she" is either Wendy Davis or Debbie, and either way, the answer is "yes," at least when I left.

"They're a mess," I say. "I've only ever seen anything like it when I've been to UT games. Everybody on one team hates everybody on the other." I think of Cassie, who defended Wendy Davis, and I add, "For the most part, anyway."

"The 'other team' is trying to roll women's rights back to the 1950s," Shireen mutters.

"The '50s sucked," Mr. Monaghan—Sean—says. "Everything was fucked after the war. For women and for men—and usually for the same reason. If I have to show up to remind them of that, I'll do it. In my fashionable orange T-shirt."

Shireen and I both laugh at that. It feels weird.

"I don't know why it has to be such a fight," I say. "Everybody here is trying to do something good, right? They just have different ideas about what that is."

"There's no understanding because the disagreement is fundamental," Shireen says to me. "Either you trust people to make their own decisions, or you don't. And if you don't, then what can I say except 'fuck you' to that? And it's the same on the other side—if you think that little pile of cells is a baby, then it's murder to kill it. How are you going to come to an understanding on something like that?"

"I just think there's a way to talk about it that is, like, way less angry—" I start, but she cuts me off.

"Things aren't always just going to be *cool*, Alex," she snaps. "Sometimes people have to fight, and you can't just ghost on it."

I open my mouth to argue, but Mr. Monaghan talks first. "Damn right," he says, even though he doesn't know that we're not exactly talking about the protests at the Capitol anymore.

I slump in my seat. I don't know who's right, or how on earth a person is even supposed to be able to tell. All I know is that when I woke up this morning,

I didn't expect to have to think about any of this. Now, suddenly, it's like there's a war going on, and I have no idea which side I'm on.

12:41 pm

When we get back to the Capitol, Shireen's great parking space is gone. In its place is a white sedan with a bumper sticker that reads "Abortion Stops a Beating Heart." Talk about adding insult to injury.

Shireen drives around the Capitol, but the street parking is full.

"I'll just drive up like an Uber driver, I guess, and you can get out," she says to me and Mr. Monaghan.

"Pull up over on the east entrance," I say as we approach. I've already texted Debbie to let her know where to meet her dad.

"Debbie's coming out this way," I say to Mr. Monaghan. "She's in orange." Not that that helps her stand out in this crowd—but I spot her on the street, craning her neck looking for whichever car is Shireen's.

"Why don't you just walk him in?" Shireen says, eager to get rid of me.

That sounds fine to me, but Mr. Monaghan gives me a look and then shakes his head, emphatic.

"I can do it," he says to Shireen. "Good to meet you, young lady." Then, turning to me, he says, "I'll see you kids inside," and winks.

Ohhhh. He thinks *Shireen* is the girl who invited me to the Capitol. Gross.

He gets out, and his daughter grabs him by the arm and leads him toward the building. Mercifully, Shireen either doesn't notice or chooses to ignore his super embarrassing wink. She pulls around the building in search of somewhere to park.

"When I was riding down this morning, there were a ton of spots around 17th and Trinity," I say. "It's a hike, but—"

"Yeah," she interrupts. "Good idea."

Cutting me off to say "good idea" is the nicest thing Shireen has done all day. Between that and how uncomfortable riding around in silence has been making me, now seems like a good time to address the big elephant in her newly repaired Honda Civic.

"Listen, Shireen," I start. "I just want to say—"

"Look, dude, save it," she snaps. "I don't get you. Like, at all. You're hanging out with Cassie Ramirez and showing up at the Capitol for the filibuster on *her* side? I don't have a clue who you are anymore. It's nice of you to go get Debbie's dad, and I don't really want to fight with you today. But I sure as hell don't want your apology right now."

My *apology*? I was pretty sure this was going to end with *her* apologizing to *me*, so let's strike that "get it off my chest" and replace it with "go to hell, Shireen." She doesn't know anything about Cassie, and even if I don't know who's right or wrong about abortion, *she's* the one who showed up in my life and turned everything druggy and gross.

I don't say anything, because I'll end up swearing at her like Mr. Monaghan swears at the guy who turns off the TV right before they give the clue in Final Jeopardy. We drive the last few blocks over to 17th and Trinity in silence, and she parks the car at one of the many parking spaces that are there like I said they would be. *You're welcome, Shireen.*

I walk to the parking meter and start feeding quarters into it, just because I'm in full-on "kill 'em with kindness" mode.

"Thanks," Shireen says, probably sarcastically, but I pretend not to notice. As we walk toward the Capitol, I'm still too angry to have anything to say. Two can play the "uncomfortable silence" game.

We pass the University of Texas tennis courts, which are just these random, old, crappy-looking courts on the street in the middle of downtown Austin. I can't help but start laughing as I look over at them.

Shireen looks at me like I'm having a breakdown or something, but then she starts laughing, too.

"Oh, dude," she says. "Is that—this is where—"

"Yep," I say. "It definitely is."

We both stand there for a minute, looking at this run-down tennis court where a couple of college guys in white shorts are volleying back and forth.

"That was . . ." Shireen starts, then looks at me like she remembers that she hates me. It was quite a night, though. Last year, right after Shireen got her license, her parents let her drive us all downtown, her and me and Jesse and Bobby, for the Black Keys concert at the Erwin Center. For some reason, Jesse kept going back to the concession stand and eating, like, a lot of junk food. I have no idea why he was so hungry, but he went back for corn dogs and funnel cakes and whatever other fried crap they had. After the show, it all started to disagree with him at once, and as we were walking back to the car along Trinity past the tennis courts, he turned to the rest of us and said, "Too many corn dogs!" Then he ran a few steps back, I guess so we wouldn't have to watch him puke, but the motion just made everything that much worse, and he horked, projectile-style, all through the fence and directly into the tennis courts.

Suddenly, a tennis ball slams against the fence, knocking me from my thoughts. One of the white-clad college guys walks over to pick it up. "Sorry, dude," he says.

"Do you think that guy was there the next morning?" I whisper to Shireen as he walks away.

She must have been lost in the same memory that I was because she does a faraway-sounding chuckle.

"I mean, they might have been finding chunks of corn dog and neon nacho cheese for days afterward," I say. "He sent that stuff flying."

"If only these guys had been there," she says. "They could have sent it right back to him."

I'd forgotten that Shireen can be fucking gross sometimes. It was one of the things that used to annoy me, but this joke just kills me. I start howling with laughter, right there on Trinity, five blocks away from the Capitol. Like, there are tears coming from my eyes at the image of these college dudes in crisp white tennis shorts, polo shirts, and matching visors backhanding Jesse's puke back in his face, while the riff from "Everlasting Light" plays in my head.

And then, for just a minute, the tears of laughter threaten to become real tears, as I think about Jesse. Shireen, who always did pay attention to things, notices.

While I'm doubled over in a weird laughing sob, she steps toward me and gently puts a hand on my shoulder. I stand up and wipe away any lingering tears, trying to pass them off as evidence of nothing more than how much the memory of Jesse puking that night slays me.

"Oh, man," I say. I turn toward the Capitol, regain my composure, and say something real cool, like, "Anyway, we should get back."

And Shireen turns to me, serious now, and says, "Yeah, dude. I miss him, too."

* * *

Shireen and I suffer a long, uncomfortable silence as we walk through the streets of downtown Austin. There's a steady stream of people all heading the same direction we are, almost all of them dressed in orange or blue. Mostly orange, although we pass a group of college students in blue shirts getting out of a bus. Shireen shakes her head in disgust.

"They have to bus 'em in to make it look like people in Texas want this," she mutters under her breath.

Because we're getting along now, I don't mention that it might be a bus full of people from Houston or Dallas.

We're walking along a path on the grounds of the Capitol when my phone buzzes. I pull it out and, when I see what it is, try not to smile so big that Shireen notices. It's a message from Cassie.

seats are opening up! ppl are leaving for lunch! it reads.

heading up as soon as i can, I text back.

Shireen doesn't notice—she's watching the crowd, which is so much bigger than it was when I got here this morning. If the Capitol looked like the tailgate before a football game a few hours ago, at this point it's like—actually, I don't even know. It's like something I haven't seen before. There are ten times as many people here now, and it's still early in the day.

One thing I notice, as I walk with Shireen in her "Come and Take It" T-shirt, is that the orangeshirts immediately regard her as part of the team. She gets smiles and waves and nods every few feet. Older people, especially, seem excited to see high school kids here—the grayer the hair, the more psyched they seem. One white-haired lady in an orange dress, here with who I assume is her husband (though I guess he could just be one of her silver-fox gentleman callers?) stops us.

"I can't believe you have to be out here doing this," she says. "I was sure that we were done fighting these battles in the '70s."

Shireen smiles and gives her a hug—she's a natural with adults; they love her. "Well, I appreciate you being here for my generation," she says. "I can't believe you're back out here fighting these battles, either."

The husband/gentleman caller, who's wearing an orange T-shirt, shoots me a nod like he's congratulating me for being in his club of cool, sensitive, feminist dudes. *Whatever you say, man,* I think, but I nod back anyway.

A moment later, we're in line for the metal detectors. The line is longer than this morning's, and it's hot outside. I'm sweating and miserable, but Shireen is bonding with the other oranges and doesn't seem to mind the heat. In front of us, a guy with spiky hair who doesn't look much older than we are turns around.

"Oh my god, I love your shirt," he says to her. He's got a lilt to his voice that makes me think he's not interested in girls, and she doesn't react like he's hitting on her.

"Thanks!" she says. "I made it last night."

"Well, it's awesome," he says. "You're awesome." Then, looking over to me, he adds, "You both are. Thank you for being here."

Who knew that all you needed to be deemed awesome by strangers was an orange T-shirt? My shirt is still in my bag, so I feel like an imposter. I'm glad when we reach the front of the line. Shireen, who's apparently feeling downright bubbly after all of the smiles from her fellow oranges, offers a big, sincere-sounding thank-you to the officer who screens her bag.

"Wow," I say. "Trying to get on their good side?"

"I'm genuinely grateful," she says. "It's the other side that guns down the people they disagree with, not ours."

"What was with that guy thanking you for being here, though?" I ask. "He was gay, right? This isn't his fight."

"It's everybody's fight," she says with a dismissive wave of her hand. "Abortion isn't just about women, dude. Guys need access to abortion, too. You ever get a girl pregnant before you're ready to be a dad, you'll be real glad she has that option. Plus, like, trans dudes can get pregnant. It's not just about women."

"But, like, that guy wasn't transgender," I say as we walk through the rotunda. "And he didn't seem like he was ever gonna get anybody pregnant."

"How do you know he wasn't trans?" Shireen asks. When she can tell I don't have a response, she continues. "One person's rights are everybody's rights. That's how it works."

I'm still not sure why a gay guy should be thanking a girl who is capable of actually getting pregnant for caring about abortion, but my obligation to accompany Shireen is at an end, so who cares.

"Hey," I say to her. "I'm gonna go check out what's happening in the gallery. See you later?"

She nods. "Okay, dude. Say hi to *Cassie.*"

Shireen has a hell of a way of getting under my skin. The way she said it, like I'm a jerk for wanting to see a girl, like Cassie is the one messing things up and causing problems, reminds me just how much she doesn't know about me. It doesn't matter if Shireen approves of Cassie or not—in fact, there's pretty much nothing less important to me than that. I'm going to go into the gallery, I'm going to spend the day with Cassie, I'm going to talk with her like a normal person who has normal conversations with normal girls, and Shireen can think whatever she wants to think about all of that.

I climb the stairs, feeling renewed by my resolve. Maybe I'll even ask Cassie out! That is an unreal thought—me and Cassie?—but she called me, and I showed up, and we are going to spend the next several hours getting to know each other better. I smooth my hair back and get in line for the gallery. It's only a handful of people deep, so I text Cassie. *Almost in!!*

As an officer waves me inside, I think about the blue shirt Father Mosier gave me, but I don't put it on. Shireen may be a jerk, but after being told how awesome I am by every rando in an orange T-shirt just because I walked in the doors with her, it would feel wrong to join the other team now. I'm not a blueshirt or an orangeshirt. I'm just me, and I don't know what I believe.

Cassie is easy to spot. She's not entirely by herself—she's sitting in a section full of people in blue—but she's the only person anywhere close to our age. The next youngest person has to be at least forty.

On the floor, Wendy Davis is still talking, addressing the other members of the Senate. She's explaining what happened "the other night," when a bunch of orangeshirts came to the Capitol to try to testify about the bill.

"Unfortunately, the chair of the committee hearing that testimony, at one point around 1:00 am, made a decision that no longer would testimony be accepted, in his words, 'because it had become repetitive,'" she says. Again, using one hundred words where ten would do, because I guess that's her job today.

She explains that, since those people didn't get to talk, she's going to read the testimony of thirty-one people right here and right now. Each one, she says, is about three minutes long. So that's her next hour and a half figured out, I guess.

Wendy Davis begins to read her first story, and I take the seat next to Cassie. "Hey," I whisper. "How's it going in here?"

"Oh, you know—Wendy Davis is still talking." She laughs.

"I guess I could ask you that anytime between now and midnight and that'd be your answer," I say.

"Seems like it." She sighs, then looks over at my white T-shirt. "Couldn't you find Father Mosier?"

Well, she had to ask. I'm not going to lie to her, but I don't want to tell her the truth, either—that I don't really want to be on the side against Mr. Monaghan and Debbie. Instead, I squeak out something vague to dodge the question.

"It's completely bonkers out there," I say. "Orange against blue, brother against brother, two men enter, one man leaves—from in here, you only get a glimpse of it."

Cassie forces a chuckle as she looks at me, like maybe she's skeptical. She doesn't really know me, after all. But then, she smiles like she's decided to believe me. "It sounds pretty intense. I'm glad you made it through alive."

"It'll take more than a civil war to kill me," I say. "So what's she been talking about?"

"Don't take this the wrong way, but I've barely been paying attention. I've been here for, like, two hours already, and that's a long time to listen to somebody talk. Mostly, I've been reading and playing games on my phone," Cassie says.

"*Candy Crush?*" I ask.

"*Fruit Ninja,*" she says, mock offended. "Come on, do I look like a *Candy Crush* kind of girl?"

"I honestly don't know what a *Candy Crush* kind of girl looks like."

"Well," she says, with a dramatic hair flip. "It's not me."

Lucky me, that's an excuse to look at her again. Somehow, even though she's been sitting in a crowded government building for the past two hours, she still looks great. Like, her hair is shiny, she smells good, and the little bit of makeup I can see on her face hasn't sweated off. I think about how much work girls like Cassie have to put into looking the way they do, and it makes the idea of asking her out feel silly—I rolled out of bed, grabbed a T-shirt, and slid my shoes on ten minutes before dashing out the door. Girls like Cassie don't look right next to guys like me.

Though I guess girls like Shireen—girls who cut the necks out of their T-shirts, and hang out with groups of dudes, and invest as much time in curating their playlists as I do—put a lot of work into how they look, too. Maybe being a girl just means you have to work harder at stuff like that than you do if you're a boy?

"I stand corrected," I say with mock deference. "What are you reading?"

I expect her to flash me the Bible or something—there sure are a lot of Bibles among the blueshirts—but instead it's a copy of *The Stand*, by Stephen King. "Whoa" slips out of me.

"What, girls can't like Stephen King?" Cassie teases.

"No, no, I know girls who like Stephen King," I say. "Just not, like, a lot of Catholic girls."

She smacks me in the shoulder with the book.

"I'll have you know that I've read this book seven times," she says with a laugh. "Oh gosh, is that what I am to you? Like, the weird super religious Catholic girl? Is that how people see me?"

"No, nothing like that," I say, even though I know it kind of is. "But, I mean, look around. You're the youngest person in blue here by like ninety years."

"It's not my fault that I alone understand how riveting it is to watch some lady talk for one million hours about—" She mimes falling asleep.

I didn't realize that Cassie would be funny. I take in the room, imagining that I might think back on this as a special memory: the first time Cassie and I spent together since we were in the fourth grade. What if she somehow ends up being my girlfriend? She's sitting here next to me, in an uncomfortable folding chair, with bright eyes and a smile now that she's no longer pretending to be zonked out. We're in a balcony overlooking the Senate floor, where most of the politicians are seated and probably just as bored as everybody else, while this one woman with blond hair and a white coat stands in pink sneakers.

Wendy Davis is still reading one of the testimonies someone sent in. I'm not paying attention until I notice that she's crying.

"——we were given the heartbreaking news that our daughter was not only sick, but had a terminal condition," Wendy Davis reads. "Every time that I left the house, someone would comment on my pregnancy. They asked perfectly normal questions about my due date, the gender, the name. I answered their questions as nicely as I could, and then I would turn around and burst into tears. Eventually, I stopped leaving my house."

The letter goes on to explain that this lady was at a Catholic hospital, where they told her she'd have to wait until the fetus's heart stopped before they could remove it, because otherwise the procedure would technically be an abortion. Eventually, the woman went to a different hospital and got someone else to do it, so she didn't have to carry a dying baby inside of her. If this bill were law, the letter says, that wouldn't have been an option.

"I chose to have a baby, and to bring her into this world," Wendy Davis reads. "I should be allowed to make the very personal, very private, and very painful decision as to how she leaves it."

I glance over at Cassie, to see what she thinks of this. It's such a sad story—but Cassie isn't sad. Instead, her face is red, her jaw is clenched, and her nose is wrinkled. She looks like she's fuming.

I turn to her, cautiously, because angry people make me nervous. "Are you okay?"

"That lady would have killed me," she says. "Wendy Davis is talking about how that lady should have killed me."

I have no idea what she means.

"I know you think I'm this weirdo religious girl," Cassie says. I try to protest, even though maybe she's right? But she keeps going. "But I'm not just here because I'm Catholic. It's a lot more personal than that for me. It's about my mom."

Because we were talking about fourth grade and the car accident and eating lunch in the music room earlier, I assume that she means it's because her mom and her sister died, and now she doesn't want anybody else to die.

"That makes sense," I say. I'm not sure if seven years after a car crash is too late to say "I'm sorry."

"It's not what you think," she says. "You know, my mom didn't believe in abortion. And she had a real complicated pregnancy with me. I was a preemie—born at twenty-five weeks. I spent the first four months I was alive on a ventilator. The doctors said I had a fifty-fifty chance of making it." She taps her hand on her heart for emphasis when she says that, like she's still surprised that she's here right now, like she wants me to understand what a miracle that is. "I've thought about that a lot, because when things went bad with her pregnancy, the doctors told her she should probably have an abortion. They said it would be a mercy. But she wouldn't do it. And here I am. Do you get it? I'm not just pro-life because I'm Catholic. I'm pro-life because I'm *alive.*"

I look down at the floor, where Wendy Davis is already reading another story. Cassie looks down, too.

"And she was just reading a story about how *my mother* should have killed me." Now Cassie starts crying, but they're not sad tears. They seem like hot, angry tears. She reaches into her bag and pulls out a pair of headphones and puts them in her ears. "I'm sorry. I can't even stand to listen to this right now."

There's something in the way she said "my mother" that makes me think that this isn't just about babies for her. It's like being here is her way of being closer to her mom, like it's a way to honor her. Seven years after a car accident is not even close to too late to say "I'm sorry."

But that's an empty thing to say, and Cassie

deserves more than that from me. I came in here with a blue T-shirt in my bag, and I let her believe I didn't have it, because—what? I was too scared to take a side? But here's this amazing girl, telling me a story that obviously breaks her heart, fearlessly taking a stand in a blue dress that tells most of the people here that she is their enemy. I know I need to be there for her.

I don't say anything, just reach into my bag, grab the T-shirt, and pull it on over my sweaty white tee. I look over to Cassie, expecting her to be upset that I wasn't honest with her, but she isn't. She just looks up at me, tears still in her eyes, and squeezes my hand.

1:38 pm

Wendy Davis keeps reading testimonies from the people who didn't get to talk a few nights ago. Cassie still has her earbuds in, and most of the people up here are staring at their phones, chatting quietly with the person next to them, or just, like, zoning out and staring at the wall—but I'm listening, trying to hear these stories the way that Cassie would.

I know I'm not the only person paying attention because sometimes, when Wendy Davis begins a new story, someone wearing orange starts to cry. When she reads one by somebody named Julie, a woman with short hair and an orange shirt tears up, and the two women sitting in the row behind her envelop her in a hug.

"Oh my god," I hear her say. "That's my story."

Wendy Davis reads the story of Julie's mom, who has Alzheimer's. She says she's almost grateful for it, because it keeps her mom from having to learn how far women's rights have backslid in this country in the past ten years. I know what Cassie would say to that: What about the babies' rights?

There are tears during the stories that no one in the room claims, too. Wendy Davis talks about someone who was raped back when abortion was illegal. This woman became pregnant. She'd get stopped at the grocery store by people who would congratulate her.

"They'd ask questions about her pregnancy, always reminding her that she was carrying the rapist's fetus," Wendy Davis says.

That sounds awful, but I think about it the way Cassie might, and it occurs to me——I can't imagine anybody said, "When is your fetus due?" to her, or "Is it a boy fetus or a girl fetus?" People would have asked her about the baby. In fact, I think I've heard the word *fetus* more times today than I have every other day of my life put together. How is anybody supposed to say when it's a "fetus" and when it's a "baby"? Doesn't that mean that it's always a baby?

The stories continue. Most of them are short. Some are angry and political, and some are sad and personal. Cassie stays on her phone, but I keep listening. I may not have thought about abortion at all before today, but I'm catching up pretty quickly, and it's interesting how both sides care about this so much and are so certain that they're right.

A few rows behind me, a guy in blue turns to the woman next to him and they both look at his phone. They seem excited. There's a murmur as whatever it is they're excited about makes its way through our section. A tiny woman sitting behind me with curly brown hair in a bun—Cassie told me her name is Marsha—leans down to fill us in, tapping Cassie on the shoulder so she takes her earbuds out.

"Don't get too excited," Marsha says. "But they think they may have found a way to break the filibuster."

"What?" Cassie says, excited. She grabs my arm and beams at me before turning back to Marsha. "How?"

"There's a lot of behind-the-scenes stuff that we're hearing from some people we know on Twitter. There are a lot of rules to the filibuster."

"And she's not following them?" Cassie says.

"Well, if she stops talking for five seconds, one of our senators can 'call the question' and vote on whether to allow the filibuster to continue," Marsha explains.

"Has she taken a five-second break yet?" I ask, mentally counting *one-Mississippi, two-Mississippi* with every pause Wendy Davis takes now.

"Probably," Cassie says confidently. "I mean, she's taken a lot of pauses up there."

"Five seconds is a long time, though," I say. I count it out on my fingers, muttering my Mississippis under my breath. It *does* take a while, and Cassie slumps. I'm surprised to realize I'm relieved that they can't just shut this whole thing down on a technicality. It feels important that they're talking about all of this, even if Wendy Davis is the one doing all the actual talking.

"That's not the only thing, though," Marsha says, like she's trying to cheer Cassie up. "There's also a three-strikes rule. She can talk forever, but only if it's directly on the topic of the bill—'germane' to the discussion. So she can keep reading these little letters, but she can't pick up the phone book and start reading people's names and addresses for three hours."

"Was that something she was thinking about doing?" I ask.

"Well, probably not," Cassie says, shooting me a look. "But she doesn't have ten hours' worth of letters."

"Who decides whether or not what she says is germane?" I ask.

"Well, that's the thing," Marsha says with a broad smile. "The Senate votes on it."

Cassie is barely able to restrain herself to her

library voice. "And there are more of us in the Senate than there are of them!"

"Exactly," Marsha says.

My stomach sinks when she says that. Am I rooting for Wendy Davis now? I thought she just had to talk until midnight. I didn't realize she had so many rules to follow while doing that.

"Am I alone here, or does that sound like cheating?" I ask Cassie after Marsha sits back in her seat.

"Cheating? Like, on the rules of the filibuster?" Cassie sounds genuinely confused by the question. "Who cares? Anyway, if she doesn't break the rules, she doesn't get stopped."

I can't stop myself from following up. "But the rules are made by people who want her to fail, right? So they can just kick her out for whatever. It's like if you go to a football game and the other team's coaches are also the refs."

Cassie shakes her head. "It's not the same. We're talking about babies' lives here. It's not a football game—it's life or death."

"Right," I find myself saying. I can't argue that, and I don't want to. How does anybody argue against the side that calls itself "pro-life"? I hate the idea that Cassie might be annoyed with me, and not just because I'm worried she's not going to like me anymore. I want to see it the way she does. It seems so clear and easy to say, "I'm here for the babies. Who cares about the rules?"

But I guess I do, because it feels wrong to me that instead of debating the arguments from the people whose letters Wendy Davis is reading, everyone is just counting seconds during her pauses. If this is as important as everyone says it is, shouldn't we talk about it honestly? Shouldn't the people in blue be trying to convince Debbie Monaghan that everybody deserves to be born? Shouldn't the people in orange be trying to convince Cassie that the lady who was raped shouldn't have to carry that baby if she doesn't want to?

I don't say any of this because I know Cassie doesn't want to hear it, and I guess I don't blame her—she's certainly thought about her side of this plenty. Instead, I say, "Sorry," even though I'm not sure what I'm sorry for.

"This is all super complicated and confusing," I whisper.

"The politics are, yeah," Cassie agrees gamely, before adding, "what's right and wrong here is actually pretty simple."

I nod like I agree with her.

"Friends?" I offer her my hand so we can shake on it.

"Friends," she says, taking me up on it. "And I

guess you survived the civil war down there after all?" She waves her hands at my blue shirt.

"I'm sorry. I didn't know how to tell you—it's hard wearing one of these, being surrounded by all of this." I look around at the whole gallery, which is like 450 people in orange and maybe another fifty of us here in blue. "I mean . . ." I trail off, because obviously she already knows that; she's the one who showed up in her pretty blue dress.

"I know," Cassie says, but not in a "you dumbass" way, like Shireen might have. She gives me a smile like she commiserates. "I don't tell that story very often, but I felt like I could share it with you, and I'm glad you were able to hear me."

"You're not mad?" I say, a little surprised. It'd be fair if she were. "You really are, like, the nicest human being I've ever met."

"That's me," she says with a twinge of—it's not embarrassment, exactly. Maybe exhaustion? "The nice one. Who has not had anything to eat or drink since I got into the gallery—which is actually kind of good, since there's no bathroom in here, but I meant to sneak a granola bar or something in my bag."

"Cassie Ramirez!" I say in mock outrage. "First I learn that you're a Stephen King fanatic, and now you admit that you'd break the rules laid out by the good people of Texas? I don't know you at all."

"You don't," she reminds me, smiling. "Not since the fourth-grade band room."

This is better! I feel like I'm sitting in a room with Cassie again, not sitting alone in a strange part of the Texas Capitol, surrounded by people in blue who make me feel uncomfortable.

"I don't, you're right," I say. "What do I need to know?"

"Oh gosh," she says. "That's the worst question!"

"Okay, what is it that you like so much about *The Stand*?"

She laughs. "That is a very specific question, Alex Collins. It's my favorite book. Have you read it?"

"Nope."

"I recommend it!" she says with some pep in her voice, like she's amused that this is what we're talking about. "I like it because it's about so many things. It starts out super scary, at least if you're terrified of basically everybody dying because of an engineered super-disease—"

"Yikes, spoiler alert," I interrupt.

"It's on like page two," she says. "Anyway, after that, it stops being so scary and starts being *fascinating*. Everybody who doesn't die gets a calling—good team or bad team, based on the dreams they have. The good people go and live on a farm in Nebraska, the bad people go to Las Vegas. And the bad people won't let the good ones just go ahead and live their lives."

"And you learn if you're a good person or a bad person based on where you get sent?" I ask. That sounds way easier than how it works in the real world. I'd be willing to endure a pandemic if it told me what team I should be on.

"Basically, yeah," she says. "The book's not so much about that as it's about what happens when you've got good people and bad people, and one of them has to win out."

"I'm assuming the good guys win in the end?"

"I thought you were worried about spoilers." She laughs. "So I'll just say 'probably.'"

"I'll read it," I tell her. "It sounds great."

"It's pretty good. It's also like a thousand pages long, though."

"Even better. All I'm reading this summer are really long books. I'm reading A Song of Ice and Fire—the *Game of Thrones* books," I clarify, and Cassie rolls her eyes like, duh, she knows what the *Game of Thrones* books are called. "I'm reading them to, uh, this old guy at this place——" I have no idea how to explain any of the circumstances that led me to the adult day care center to Cassie, so I don't even try. "Uh, this place I volunteer at. Mr. Monaghan. Three mornings a week."

"That's really cool," she says, with the sort of distant appreciation you might have if someone told you they collected rare stamps or practiced juggling for three hours a night. "He likes them?"

"We're kind of each other's only friends at this point," I say. It's the same joke that's been in my head all summer, but I quickly realize what a pathetic thing it is to say out loud to Cassie Ramirez. "Anyway, yeah, he's super into them. *Loves* the beheadings."

She laughs, like a snort-laugh, the kind that seems totally out of place coming from her.

"That's hilarious. And super sad," she says. "At least he likes the books!"

"At least he likes the books," I agree, relieved that she thinks it's funny instead of feeling sorry for me.

"What happened to all of your other friends?" she asks.

"What happened to *yours*?" I gesture at the old people in blue here to support her. Do I really want to get into all of this with Cassie, of all people?

"Mine are swimming," she says. "Probably. Or getting high."

"Mine too, actually," I say. Screw it. "Or they would have been, if we were still friends."

"Is that why you don't have friends anymore?" she asks, sincere this time. "Because they're all busy getting high?"

"That's the reason I don't have some of my friends anymore. I mean, it's part of it, anyway." I take a deep breath. Are we doing this?

She pushes—gently, like she cares, not nosy, like she wants gossip. "What's the other part?"

I shoot a stream of air past my lower lip over my nose. Well, heck, she told me her super personal story. I guess we are doing this.

"My first group of friends, they got all druggy." I feel compelled to add, because I'm talking to ultra-Catholic Cassie, "They're not bad people or anything, they just—I don't know—they made some bad decisions."

"It happens," she says, smiling. "I tried weed a few times, but I didn't like it. I'm not a prude about it—it's just not my thing, I guess." The idea of Cassie Ramirez smoking weed is hard to conjure, but I guess I believe her.

"I think I kind of *am* a prude about it," I say. "Which I didn't really think about until all of my friends got into it."

"All of them?" she asks.

"Well, just the first group," I say.

"And the second group?"

"They're the sort of people who would have a dream telling them to go to Las Vegas in the apocalypse," I say.

She looks at me skeptically. "That's dramatic."

"Do you know Jacob Kohler? Or Tommy Richman?" I ask.

She nods. "Oh, yeah. Football guys. I wouldn't have guessed you were friends with them. Doesn't seem like you'd have much in common."

"We don't," I say.

"Then why . . . ?"

I lean over to relay the next part. She leans in, too. I take a real deep breath. Okay, then. It's Getting Real Time with Alex Collins and Cassie Ramirez. Let's do this.

"Let me tell you a totally hypothetical, made-up story about a friend of mine. We'll call him . . . Alex," I say. I haven't told this story to anybody. Who would I tell? The one person I most want to talk to is gone.

"One day, Alex realizes that the friends he's had since he was little are all way too busy getting high and drunk for him to feel comfortable hanging out with them anymore, and it makes him really sad. But he's got a part-time job, in the glamorous field of pizza production, at a neighborhood retailer, where he slings 'za, as they call it in the biz, three or four days a week. And among his coworkers in the 'za-slinging business are Jacob and Tommy. Jacob and Tommy are—to put it bluntly—jerks. But Alex finds himself working late with them one night. They're making fun of Alex's old friends, which is something they do a lot, because Alex's old friends are the sort of kids who wear black nail polish to school or do whatever other things offend the Jacob Kohlers and Tommy Richmans of the world. They're friendly enough toward Alex, although he suspects that they say awful things about him when he's not there. This particular evening, when Alex hears them talk about what losers Jesse Quinones and his friends are, he doesn't slip away uncomfortably. Instead, he sticks around and joins in. And, to his surprise, it feels kind of good to say these mean things about his old friends."

I look over at Cassie now, to see her reaction. I feel really exposed talking about this here, of all places—in the Texas State Senate gallery, overlooking the Senate floor, where Wendy Davis is still reading the stories of people who wrote her letters describing their abortions.

"I knew that you and Jesse Quinones were close," Cassie says, softly and sympathetically. "I'm really sorry."

I nod, not meeting her eyes. I don't feel right accepting condolences, especially right now. I don't like thinking about how Jesse dying must have been gossip among people who didn't know him. It all feels too big, so I just keep going with my story.

"Alex starts hanging out with Jacob and Tommy.

And it's fun, at first. After work, they go to Jacob's house sometimes to play poker, or to the mall. He didn't do that with his old friends, just like his new friends don't spend much time listening to music or making jokes over bad horror movies. When they play poker, they invite other guys over and talk, like, 'guy talk.' Everybody acts like Jacob is the smartest guy in the room—like he's Jaime Lannister, or whoever that sort of character is in *The Stand*. They treat everything he says like it's worthy of being etched in marble."

Cassie looks at me again, but now with concern. "It sounds like you—" I duck my head, shaking it, and she starts again. "It sounds like your friend Alex didn't think much of these guys. Why hang out with people you—he—didn't like?"

I shrug. "Well, what else was he going to do? Hang out at the old folks' home reading *A Game of Thrones* to an ornery World War II vet?"

"It doesn't sound that bad," she says.

"Well, it wasn't my first choice," I say.

She nods and meets my eyes. Her face is kind, sympathetic, and easy to talk to. I keep expecting her to say I'm on my way to Las Vegas and be done with me, but she just keeps encouraging me to go on.

"Anyway," I say. "All is going—I don't know if I'd say that it's going *well*, but all is certainly *going*—for our friend Alex. And then one night, after work, he gets invited along with Jacob and Tommy as, they tell him, they're going to do something super fun."

This part of the story is hard to talk about. I feel ashamed and awful just thinking about it. Cassie puts her hand on mine for a moment, like she can tell how much this sucks to talk about. I'm sure she can. I'm sure it's written all over my face.

After taking a moment to regain my composure, I continue. "So I'm not—Alex isn't a great driver, but they ask him if he wants to drive Jacob's Mustang that night, and he says sure, okay, whatever they're doing sounds good, he likes to do things that are super fun. They give him directions for where to go, and as he drives through the neighborhood north of UT, he realizes where he's heading: to his old friend Jesse Quinones's house."

I can't believe I'm telling Cassie about this. I haven't gone to confession in years, but here's a great idea—instead of to a priest, I'll go confess the worst thing I've ever done to the prettiest girl I've ever met.

As I continue with the story, I keep my voice down because I'm scared that that Marsha lady is listening in. I know I'm being ridiculous—there's no way she cares about some high school drama—but I can't help myself. I don't want to look at Cassie's face as I'm telling her this, so I don't.

"As he's driving there, does Alex say, 'Hey, this is a bad idea' to Jacob and Tommy? No," I say, "he does not. Does he ask, 'Uh, guys, what is it we're going to *do*?' No, again, he does not. Because he doesn't want to know. Because it's easier to just keep driving. So he does, and he follows the directions as Jacob reads them off his phone—left here, left here, right here, stop here. And, sure enough, he stops the car in front of Jesse Quinones's house, where the driveway is full of cars belonging to Jesse's friends. Alex can see them in the garage apartment they like to hang out in, with the TV flickering. He turns off the headlights so they won't get caught—because, man, how awful would *that* be, to get caught?—and Jacob and Tommy hop out of the car. Jacob pops the trunk and grabs a big utility brick, and Tommy grabs a can of red house paint. Jacob throws his brick through the back windshield of Jesse's girlfriend's car, and Tommy dumps a gallon of red paint all over it, and the driveway, and Jesse's mom's car, and they get back in the Mustang, and Alex peels out and drives away as the car alarm starts blaring and the lights in the garage apartment come on."

"Oh my gosh," Cassie says, and I'm certain that whatever sympathy I had imagined in her eyes has been replaced by scorn. But when I rub my face and look at her, she just seems curious. "I remember that

Jacob and Tommy got in trouble—that was a whole thing—but I never heard about you being a part of whatever happened."

I nod. "Well, I didn't throw a brick, or pour any paint on anything. And I wouldn't have if they'd asked me to. I'm not proud of what I did, but I know where my line is. The next morning, I called Mrs. Quinones, and I told her what happened."

"Wow," Cassie says, like she admires that. Maybe Cassie really is *too* nice. I don't deserve admiration for this.

"I mean, I had to," I explain. "This was *awful,* Cassie. These were my *friends.* We may not have been hanging out anymore, and I may have had some hard feelings—but a few months earlier, I'd have *been there* that night. I couldn't talk to Jesse about it, or Shireen—his girlfriend, whose car got smashed up—but I needed to tell somebody who could make it right. So I called his mom and told her, and she asked me if I'd go to the police station, which I did. And since I didn't do any of the damage myself, and I didn't even know what was going to happen when we got to Jesse's house, I got a deferred prosecution deal—basically if I do community service and stay out of trouble, I don't get anything on my record. The police told me to make some new friends, and

Mrs. Quinones gave me a hug when we left, which made me feel worse."

"Why?" Cassie asks.

This is the worst part, but she's been listening to me for so long that I owe her an answer.

"Because she was treating me like I was still this good kid who came over to her house to draw and listen to music and eat her cookies," I say. "And I wasn't. Not only that, none of us were those good kids anymore—not me, not Jesse, not Shireen or his other friends—and I don't think she had any idea. I felt like I should tell her that—that things in the garage apartment were progressing way past beer and weed—but I didn't know how."

Cassie grabs my hand again and squeezes. Jesse's death was the hottest topic of gossip back in March. I don't get the impression that Cassie is into the rumor mill, but I have to assume she knows what happened to him. Either way, I can't bring myself to say the words.

"I couldn't stand the thought of betraying Jesse a second time," I tell her, finally. "But I really should have."

3:31 pm

As I finish spilling this story about my "friend," I feel like a big, raw wound of a person. I can't believe I've told my darkest secret to this pretty girl who asked me to meet her here since she thought I was a good person because I was accidentally nice to her on a really bad day she had when we were ten years old. I don't realize where I am at all, until I hear a voice that isn't the mild droning of Wendy Davis speak from the Senate floor.

A thin-haired blond dude who David Dewhurst refers to as "the senator from Hunt County" just stood up. David Dewhurst asks Wendy Davis if she'll yield to this guy, whose name is Senator Deuell. She sways on her feet—she must be friggin' *exhausted* right now, after talking nonstop with no break longer than five seconds for the past four hours—but she responds, "I'm happy to answer your questions, Senator Deuell, but in doing so, I will not yield the floor."

Once that's settled, Senator Deuell starts

asking her a question, and Cassie shakes her head in disapproval.

"What's going on down there?" I ask her.

She purses her lips. "I have no idea what he's doing. He's helping her, basically."

"Really? Why would he do that?" I ask.

"To hear himself talk." Cassie looks behind her to the grown-up blues, to see if anybody can clarify.

"Deuell is one of the good ones," Marsha chimes in as she leans down toward us. "He's going to let her have it here, watch."

"I don't know why that matters," Cassie says. "He's giving her a break."

I remember Cassie saying this morning that the other Democrats in the Senate could give Wendy Davis a break by interrupting her for questions, which makes this even *more* confusing—why haven't they been doing that before now?

"Dewhurst wasn't letting her take questions until now," Cassie explains. "He refused to recognize them to speak, which is what should be happening now if we want to win." She turns to me, seeming annoyed at pretty much everything, including me. "I hope *that's* not cheating, too?"

I have no idea if it's cheating or not. I guess it's Wendy Davis's filibuster, so she should do all the talking? Everything new that happens here just reminds me of the short list of things I'm an expert on—screwing over your friends, World War II–era nautical curse words, the Stark family lineage in *A Game of Thrones*—and that the minutiae of the Texas Senate rulebook isn't on it.

Despite all the listening I've been doing since I got into the gallery, abortion isn't on that list either, which makes the actual conversation happening on the Senate floor hard to follow. Basically, Senator Deuell is talking about how sad all of the stories are, but they're also from people who say that they got called degrading things for having abortions, and he wants to know if Wendy Davis thinks that the bill they're trying to pass is degrading in the same way—as if all his side wants to do is make things safer for the people who get abortions and no one on his side would ever say anything that might possibly make someone feel bad for getting one.

"I don't get it," I say to Cassie. "Is he saying that he doesn't think that people get heated and call each other names when they're talking about abortion? Because when I was outside earlier, I saw some guy call a girl a 'cheerleader of death,' and she started screaming 'Hail Satan' at people singing 'Amazing Grace.' It sounds like *everybody* is rude about it."

"She said 'Hail Satan'?" Cassie says. "Holy cow."

"I guess, yeah." It sounded to me like the girl was

being sarcastic or trying to get a rise out of people, but the way Cassie says it, it's like she assumes the girl was possessed by the devil. "But is this guy saying that he doesn't think people should take it personally? Because it all seems very personal."

"Of course it's personal," Cassie says. "We're talking about babies' lives."

I guess it really could be that simple? I know Cassie is here because the thing she cares the most about is the babies who get aborted. But I also know Shireen is downstairs in an orange T-shirt because she believes that all of this is a fight for women's rights, and restricting abortion is like telling her personally that she's not allowed to make her own decisions. That's such a fundamental disagreement that I guess it makes sense that whenever you put them in the same place, the orangeshirts and the blueshirts start hissing at each other.

On the floor, Wendy Davis says that she'll answer Senator Deuell's question about how the bill *is* degrading to women who are trying to get abortions. She says she'll start with the "ambulatory surgical center requirements," and again, it seems like she's trying to use seventeen words when three would do the trick. Then she says something that starts to get at the thing that's been gnawing at me in all of this—about honesty and cheating and how nobody seems to be debating the actual things they say they care about. She says that there are forty-two abortion clinics in Texas, and only five of them are "ambulatory surgical centers," and the bill will require all of the ones that aren't to close. She says that she's asked the Republican senators why that would make abortions safer, which is supposed to be the point of the bill, but nobody's been able to give her an answer. Nobody's been able to say what's so unsafe about abortions right now that they need to pass a law that'll close all the clinics that don't meet its requirements. She says that even though they're pretending that this is about making abortion safer, she doesn't think it'll do jack about that—and that they're only pretending to care about safety because the Constitution says that they can't ban abortion outright.

"Could it be," she says about the real motive behind all of the language on safety, "might it just be a desire to limit women's access to safe, healthy, legal, Constitutionally protected abortions in the state of Texas?"

I lean forward to hear Senator Deuell answer, for him to say that this is about saving babies, the way that Cassie would.

But he doesn't. Instead, he blames Twitter for Wendy Davis thinking that and asks her if she *really* believes that her fellow senators would try to limit Texans' access to safe, healthy, legal abortions. I glance over at Cassie, who still seems annoyed that this guy is giving Wendy Davis something to do besides drone on and on for the next eight hours. But I think she should be annoyed because this guy is a liar. Wendy Davis *should* believe that her fellow senators would do that, since that's what Cassie and all of her—our?—fellow blueshirts are counting on. Why can't this guy just tell the truth?

As their conversation continues, it all feels exhausting, watching these people lie to each other, or talk past each other, or not listen to each other. Still, there's one other thing that sticks with me. When Wendy Davis asked Deuell how this bill will do anything to protect Texas women, I couldn't help noticing that he couldn't give her an answer.

3:52 pm

So David Dewhurst just threatened to throw us all in jail. Things got weird here after Wendy Davis and Senator Deuell started trading questions and answers—at one point, she called out David Dewhurst himself for "abusing the power he's been entrusted with." Dewhurst got all defensive, and the entire gallery erupted into applause, except the section I'm sitting in, which was mostly full of people in blue shaking their heads at the outburst.

Everybody quieted down, and then some senator asked him to read out loud what the punishment would be for "obstructing" the proceedings by being annoying—and guess what? It's *jail*. He can put anybody who is "disrespectful" or "disorderly" in jail for forty-eight hours. Wouldn't my mom be shocked if I skated out of jail time on charges of property destruction and vandalism, then went to jail for watching the State Senate with Cassie Ramirez?

Anyway, after we've been duly warned, Wendy

Davis and the senator from Hunt County keep going on to hear themselves talk, which makes sense for her since she has to keep going till midnight, but not much sense for him, since—like Cassie said earlier—he wants her to stop talking.

Does "disorderly conduct" include leaning over to talk to Cassie? I decide to chance it.

"Riveting stuff," I say, nodding down toward the blathering between our esteemed state senators.

"Oh, totally," she says. "I was dying to know what page five, line one of this bill says, so I'm really glad he took the time to read it out loud to everybody here."

"You sound cranky. Are you sure you don't have a granola bar in there?" I gesture to her bag.

"Don't even talk about food unless you have an apple for me."

"If I'd known . . ." I sigh. "But alas, nothing to chew but my fingernails over the suspense of whether one of them is going to misquote some statistic by a tenth of a percent. On the bright side, I just remembered that they *do* have a pretty good cafeteria in the Capitol, so we could sneak out and actually get a proper snack."

"I wish," she says. "I really do."

"Are you not going to eat at all today?" I ask.

"When she's done," Cassie says firmly. "If Wendy

Davis is going to stand up there and not eat anything or go to the bathroom for what she believes in, I can do the same."

Damn. Where do they even *make* girls like Cassie?

Most of my friends have made indulging yourself sound cool—even before things got druggy, we'd brag about downing Red Bulls or Mountain Dew and playing *Mass Effect 3* for an entire weekend—but she's out here sounding like a badass for not eating lunch. All of our "dude, I totally stayed up all night finding all the Riddler trophies in *Arkham City*" bragging seems pretty empty.

I want to tell her how amazing that is, but I can't even imagine how I would do that without sounding awkward. Instead, I start chewing on the side of my hand like it's a delicious ear of corn on the cob.

This gets a smile out of her, which is satisfying in its own way.

"Oh, man, a handwich!" she says. "I should have thought of that."

"I'm full of good ideas," I say.

"You don't have to stay here the whole time, you know." She gets a vaguely apologetic look on her face. "I mean, if you want to get food or something."

I look at her, my face drawn in mock hurt. "Are you trying to get rid of me, Cassie?"

"Oh, heck no. I'm grateful for this diversion from

post-apocalyptic horror. And from *The Stand*." She does a little *ba-dum-ching* noise and an air drum routine, before gesturing to the Senate floor and the post-apocalyptic horror that is this endless question-and-answer session about nothing.

I look at her with a weird smile.

Apparently, she can see the wheels turning in my head, because she nudges me hard with her shoulder. "Whaaaaaat?"

"You're a *dork*," I blurt.

"Look who's talking," she says in mock offense.

"No, no, sorry. I didn't mean anything by it. I just—you know how it is. You see somebody in school or with their friends from a distance, and you get an idea about who they are. And then you spend a few hours with them one afternoon, and you realize— wow, this is a person who seriously still does that 'ba-dum-ching' noise when she makes a bad joke."

"You thought that joke was bad?" she asks through faux tears. I return an exaggerated grimace and a big hate-to-admit-it shrug. She laughs. "No, though, I get it. We all have preconceived notions about who people are. I had these ideas about you that I just kind of held on to from grade school."

It blows my mind that Cassie thought about me at all over the past few years. Whatever she thought I was, though, I've shattered it by telling her about

Jacob and Tommy and Jesse. I couldn't even be honest about whether I got a blue T-shirt from Father Mosier.

She must read that I feel weird about what she said, because she goes on to clarify. "Everybody tells me I'm 'nice.' Like, you said that yourself. And that's what I thought about you in the music room: just, like, this really simplified version of a nice guy. But that's not all you are—you're complex, and interesting."

Oh no, I can feel my face getting so red that I probably look like I'm having a stroke. I keep my mouth shut and hope she doesn't notice.

"It's better to know that stuff," she finishes. "Even if it means your dorkiness comes out, too."

My face is still a fire engine, but I really do need to say something. "You're not *just* a dork. You have really weird taste in books, too."

Great move, Alex. You're killing it here.

She smiles, though, and I realize—not for the first time today—that I am really not on Cassie's level. But how many people are?

I've been confused all day that Cassie doesn't have an army of friends who'd show up at the Capitol to wear blue T-shirts and dick around on their phones in the gallery with her just because she asked. I can't imagine why anybody *wouldn't* want to be around

Cassie as much as possible—but I guess everything that makes her so amazing isn't necessarily what the other kids at McCallum High School want from a girl like Cassie Ramirez.

A guy on Wendy Davis's side of the aisle, with black hair gelled into what looks like a bulletproof helmet, interrupts the ongoing blah-blah-blah to ask if Wendy Davis will yield. She says she won't yield the floor, but he can go ahead and speak.

Behind us, Marsha starts shaking her head, looking like she wants to spit on the ground.

"You know, God gave us the opportunity to end this last night," she says. "But then Eddie Lucio there—who's supposed to be on our side, even though he's a Democrat, because he's a Catholic—he screwed it up."

"What happened?" Cassie asks.

"There was a procedural vote yesterday," Marsha explains. "If we'd won it, we could have held the vote on the bill last night and skipped the debate, which is where the filibuster happens—because last night, we had enough votes to pass the bill," she says. "But Lucio switched sides on the procedural vote, and now we have to sit through all of this."

"That's super weird," I say. "Why did he switch sides yesterday?"

"Well," Marsha says, "the Senate was down a

member last night, when we called for the vote. One of the Dems wasn't here, so Lucio voted to side with her."

"How did a senator skip showing up for this? There are literally thousands of people here right now, and none of *us* are senators." I gesture to the gallery.

Cassie kind of shrugs and rubs her eyes. "It was Senator Van de Putte. Her dad died in a car accident last week, and last night was the wake," she says softly.

I get that sinking-stomach feeling again, like I'm cheering for the team that's willing to cheat to win. "Wait a second. They called for a vote to pass this, and they made her choose between being here or being at *her dad's wake?*"

Cassie keeps looking at the Senate floor. "Yeah. I mean, I get it. I know what it's like to lose a parent in a car accident."

I guess she does—but at least nobody tried to make her miss being there with her family. Missing a funeral you know you should have been at is something I know about, but I don't say that to her.

"That's why he voted with them last night, I guess," Cassie says. "I don't know what I'd have done—but we're talking about babies here. I think I'd do whatever it takes to save them."

On the Senate floor, Eddie Lucio is talking about just that.

"I did it because it was the right thing to do," he says. He goes on to talk about the letters that Wendy Davis had been reading. "The letters were heartfelt, and I cried inside when you were crying because of the hardships that women face in this world. But I also thought about the fifty-six million babies that would never be born, would never be able to write a letter to their legislators, talking about how they felt about life, and how grateful they might have been for their mothers to be giving them that opportunity."

Cassie digs her elbow into my side. "See? That's what I'm talking about. This wouldn't even be happening at all if all of those babies could vote."

I don't say what I'm thinking, which is *How do you know that they'd be on your side?* Instead, I just listen to Wendy Davis, who lays it on thick, talking about her respect and admiration for Senator Lucio.

Then she says, "I'm sorry that we disagree on this particular issue. I think that, by your very comments, your hope for what this bill would achieve is that *abortion service would decrease in Texas.*" She stresses this part like it's important. "I don't think that's been the stated purpose for this bill. It's been stated that it's to make women who are having an abortion safer, and to provide better health care."

I try to keep my face neutral for Cassie's sake, but I can't help but cheer a little bit on the inside when she says this. *Thank you, Wendy Davis.* Cassie isn't here talking about how women who get abortions in Texas are at risk from a dangerous procedure. She's here because if her mom had had an abortion, she wouldn't be alive. I'll put on a blue shirt to support her on that, but I don't know why that blue shirt says "Protect Texas Women" instead of "Save Texas Babies." Why is this Eddie Lucio guy the only senator talking about the fifty-six million babies who will never be born? Why is Cassie supporting the senators when they say they want abortions to happen in ambulatory surgical centers, whatever those are, when she's here because she doesn't want abortions to happen *anywhere*?

"I like this guy," I say to her. "Why does everybody else talk about making abortions safer, instead of just making them illegal?"

"I mean, the Supreme Court ruled in *Roe v. Wade* that abortion is a right in the Constitution," she says. "I don't know where they found that in the Constitution, but that's how it works. So, because of that, they can't just pass laws that make it harder to get abortions. They have to find a way to get around that, and the best way to do it is to pass laws that they can say are to make abortions safer—and if that makes abortions harder to get, then that's just, like, a *side effect*." She stresses those last few words like they're in air quotes.

"Doesn't—I don't know. Isn't that basically lying to everybody, though?" I finally come out and say. "Like, if they're trying to close abortion clinics and make it so there are fewer abortions in Texas, aren't they just *lying* when they say 'Protect Texas Women'?" I point in the general direction of Marsha's shirt.

"If the babies got to grow up, half of them would be Texas women, too," Cassie says. "That's the whole thing. I don't get why you're so hung up on all the political stuff. Politics are the tool, and politics are just crappy."

It's the closest I've heard Cassie come to swearing. She's getting fired up, shout-whispering as she talks about all of this.

"I don't care about politics. If they have to play a game where they have to say 'protect women's health' instead of 'protect babies' lives' in order to do the right thing, then play the game! I'm here for them"—she gestures to the air or something, wherever the babies are—"not for *them*." She points now to the Senate floor. "If they have to play the politics game to save babies, who cares? The baby who was gonna get murdered, but who gets to live instead? I think she'll forgive us."

I can't argue with what Cassie is saying, but I know that if Debbie Monaghan were here, she would be able to. I don't care about politics, but this has to be a real debate or it's all just a bunch of people lying about why they're doing what they're doing. I just want people to be honest in all of this so everybody here gets to have their voice heard. Whoever says it best should get to win.

Wendy Davis has been talking for hours and hours at this point—she's answered questions from the other senators, she's read even *more* letters from people who all are saying basically the same thing, and she's read articles from the newspapers in Austin and Houston about "women's health" and abortion. I'm barely listening as she reads from another article about abortion, but Marsha stands up, excited, when a bald senator who looks like a creepy Santa Claus with his bushy white beard stands up.

"Oh, he's gonna do it," she says. "Watch this—this is the next move in shutting this down."

She speaks with self-righteous confidence, like she's so right she's gonna dunk all over anybody who disagrees with her. It reminds me of how Jacob Kohler would talk to Tommy Richman when he was trying to bluff him out during a game of poker.

David Dewhurst interrupts Wendy Davis to address Senator Creepy Santa. "Senator Nichols. For what purpose do you rise?"

Wendy Davis stops reading out loud about Planned Parenthood funding, and Nichols grins.

"Mr. President, under Rule 4.03, is the budget germane to this bill?" he asks.

"No," David Dewhurst says, with what seems like relish.

Nichols nods. "I think she's talking about the budget."

5:48 pm

After Senator Santa says the word *germane*, the room changes. It's subtle, but things grow tense: The orangeshirts lean forward in their seats, nervous. The blueshirts in my section sit with satisfied smiles, like the plan is underway. On the Senate floor, one of Wendy Davis's fellow Democratic senators moves to stand behind her, while she explains why she started talking about funding for Planned Parenthood.

I recognize the senator standing behind her. Kirk Watson is famous—or at least infamous—in Austin. He has thin white hair and an aw-shucks smile. He became a meme when I was about twelve years old because he sounded like an ignorant Texas bumpkin on CNN, and the CNN guy started making fun of him.

Wendy Davis says why she thinks what she was reading was relevant to the bill—that during the debate over the bill, she'd talked about the same thing, and nobody had said jack then, and anyway, it's a bill about abortion and Planned Parenthood's funding got pulled a couple years ago because the Senate doesn't like abortion. When she finishes, David Dewhurst turns to talk to the lady behind him, who has dark hair and wears a white suit.

I nudge Cassie. "Who's that?"

She shakes her head and throws up her hands.

"That's the parliamentarian." Marsha leans down to explain to both of us. "She's kind of like the referee when it comes to the rules of the Senate."

After a moment of consulting the parliamentarian, Dewhurst leans toward his microphone to address Wendy Davis.

"Senator, I don't think that the contents and the subject matter of the funding of Planned Parenthood is germane to this debate. Please consider this as a warning," he says. "And if you could, keep your comments to Senate Bill 5, the elements in the bill, and the subject of abortion."

I want to be on Cassie's side here, so I think again about what she said. *Politics are the tool to save the babies.* That matters, I tell myself. And I know it does. Would I break some rules to save someone's life? Of course I would. Death is so final and terrible. I would have broken a million rules, big or small, to save Jesse.

I have to tell myself that, because otherwise, it

sure seems like talking about Planned Parenthood *is* talking on the subject of abortion. I look over at Cassie, who gives me a big "I don't care how it happens" smile. Meanwhile, there's murmuring among the oranges in the room. I imagine what all of this must feel like to Shireen and Debbie Monaghan and the people downstairs, who believe in their side just as much as Cassie does hers.

Wendy Davis starts talking again. This time, she says, she'll be speaking about alternatives to abortion. She talks for a minute before, once again, Evil Santa stands up.

"Senator Nichols, for what purpose do you rise?" David Dewhurst asks him.

"To call a question of a point of order on Rule 4.03, on the germaneness," he says. "I don't think alternatives to abortion are related to Senate Bill 5."

The air sucks out of the entire room as Dewhurst turns to the parliamentarian again. The oranges gasp, while the blues sit at the edge of their seats in anticipation.

"Strike two!" Marsha gloats.

What the hell? They literally just told Wendy Davis that talking about abortion is okay, and now they're gonna give her another strike for talking about abortion? I look back at Marsha and see Jacob Kohler's smile on her face.

I would have broken a million rules to save Jesse, but the rules weren't the problem. It was the dishonesty. If I had just been honest with his mom, he might still be here. I didn't want to betray him by telling somebody the truth, but this dishonesty doesn't get anybody anywhere. Here's Marsha, proudly beaming because she's on the team with the best liars. But if they can just do whatever the hell they want, and lie about what the rules are when it suits them, then what is anybody even doing here?

Maybe politics is a game, but if it's rigged, then one side is always going to lose, and I care about the people on that side, too. I keep my eyes on the Senate floor, watching Dewhurst and the parliamentarian, just because I don't want to look at Cassie and see her celebrating the way that Marsha is.

Finally, Dewhurst responds. He says that, as long as they're talking about abortion, it's okay for now, but he'll revisit that question later. Now Marsha is the one who's pouting, and the oranges, who've all been holding their breath—like I have, I realize—finally exhale.

Cassie must see the relief on my face. "Wait," she says. "Are you on her side now?"

I take a deep breath. "Look, I'm new to all of this. To, like, politics and abortion and everything we're here for. I don't really know what I think—but it has to be honest. It has to be a debate. It sucks that they're lying about what they want and cheating about what the rules are to make sure that doesn't get to happen."

"Even if——while you're busy debating——babies are dying?" Cassie sounds incredulous, like she genuinely doesn't understand.

I look down at the Senate floor again to avoid the perfect "I'm not mad, I'm just disappointed" look on her face.

"I don't know," I admit. "You know Debbie Monaghan from church? She's downstairs. She's wearing orange and has a big sign that says 'God Is Pro-Choice.' Her dad, the old guy I read to, he's here, and he's wearing orange, too." I leave Shireen out of it. "I don't want to let you down, but all I know is that you're a good person, and Mr. Monaghan is a good person, and Debbie is a good person, and you all believe different things. So I need to figure out what *I* believe."

I feel good saying all of that. I hope Cassie will respect that I'm being honest with her——but she mostly just looks hurt.

"If you don't even know what you believe," she says, "why did you even come here today?"

What am I supposed to say? *I'm here because I think you're really pretty, and a long time ago, you*

*were nice to me when everybody else was mean to me,
and I came up into the gallery because I was hoping
that somehow by the end of all of this you'd maybe
want to be my girlfriend?*

Of course I can't say any of that—but because
I'm silently thinking it, my face starts heating up,
and Cassie realizes what the answer is anyway.

"Oh," she says. This time I do look at her because
I'm curious what Cassie Ramirez looks like when she
feels completely betrayed. "You're here to, what,
to hit on me?" She doesn't even sound angry, just
really hurt.

"I—I mean—I'm not—" I rack my brain, like
I might have a good answer hiding somewhere. But
of course I don't.

Cassie looks at me like I'm some pathetic creep
she told her secrets to because she thought she could
trust him. "I don't think you believe in anything. I
thought you were a really good guy, but I guess that
was just someone I thought I knew a long time ago."

Hearing her say that stings so bad that I want
to shrink down to subatomic size and crawl through
the fibers of the carpeting on my way to the ledge of
the balcony, where I will plummet to my microscopic
death. I want to argue with her, to defend myself, but
I don't even know what I would say. I try to imagine
a way to take this all back, to say, "You're right, I'm

sorry," but I can't find those words, either. And then it's too late.

"You need to go," she says. "I want to hold this seat for someone who's on my side."

That's fair, I guess. Of course she wants that, and as much as I want to be that, I guess I can't be.

I take my blue T-shirt off and stuff it in my bag, and then I get the hell out of the Texas Senate gallery.

6:01 pm

Well, shit.

I pause outside the gallery, feeling like a total jerk. Couldn't I have just kept my mouth shut and supported her in this thing that she obviously knows more about than I do? Couldn't I have just been there for her?

But I guess not. I don't know why, but thinking about Jesse in there got me thinking about Shireen in her orange shirt downstairs and how this is all too important to too many people to just join a side because the girl I like is on it.

It's *loud* outside the gallery, like the minutes before a school assembly when no one has shushed us yet. Cassie and I were talking in stage whispers inside, but if we'd been out here, we'd have been shouting in each other's ears.

The line to get inside the gallery is long—longer even than it was this morning. It's still going to take a while before Cassie's spare seat finds a new occupant, though, if the unofficial rule that oranges sit with oranges and blues sit with blues holds—almost all of the people waiting to get in are wearing orange. I hope that the bluest of blue people comes in and sits next to her, and that Cassie and Marsha and their new Smurfy pal all get to celebrate whatever the Texas Senate does together. I just can't sit with them while they do it.

I don't know where I'm going now, but I'm not going home, not after all of that. I wind my way down the line like I'm swimming upstream. When I get to the elevators, I join three orangeshirts who are already standing outside the doors.

"Come on, come on, come on," a guy with spiky hair and a UT football jersey says as he taps his foot impatiently.

"They're not going to kill the filibuster before you get to the auditorium," his friend, a woman with black bangs and a vintage orange dress, says.

"This is so messed up," he says as the light dings and the doors open. I get in with them, glad to be reminded about the auditorium.

The elevator stops at the ground floor of the rotunda, before the subbasements. It's *really* loud now. I peek my head out of the elevator to take a look.

However crowded the place seemed earlier, I'm starting to get a sense of what a *really* crowded room is like—it's like being at a concert or something, where you can't even walk without bumping into somebody. I look at my watch and realize that it's after six o'clock. This must be the after-work crowd—and most of them are orange. In fact, it seems like the size of the crowd has doubled, and everybody who showed up is wearing orange. The blues were outnumbered before, but this is bonkers.

We get to the subbasement where the auditorium is, and I bounce out of the elevator, weaving through people on my way. The hall outside the auditorium is crowded, too, but at least it still feels like a functional hallway. I walk into the room. There are a few scattered seats, but my butt is sore from being in the gallery, so I stand near the back.

On the screen, the filibuster continues—I think—but Wendy Davis isn't the one talking. Instead, it's Kirk Watson. He's asking a lot of questions—long-winded ones, at that—and she's giving short answers like "correct" to most of them. Basically, it sounds like he's rephrasing her points from earlier in the filibuster in as wordy a way as he can, then turning to her once a minute or so to ask, "Is that what you're saying?" Cassie mentioned that they might do this to give Wendy Davis a rest.

"What you're saying is the Constitutional underpinning of *Roe v. Wade* was that it invaded a right that a woman possessed, based on the concept of personal liberty," Kirk Watson says. "And it's your understanding that what the court found was that personal liberty is embodied in the Fourteenth Amendment's due process clause?"

"That's correct," Wendy Davis says.

Watson goes on with another question that isn't really a question. In the back of the Senate Chamber, a bald head with a white beard appears on the screen.

"Senator Nichols, for what purpose do you rise, sir?" David Dewhurst asks.

Nichols says the word *germane*, and the auditorium gets angry. A lady near the front stands up and stomps her foot. People start booing the screen. Other people yell "Shut up!" either at them or at Senator Nichols or just at, like, everybody. After being in the Senate gallery, where we were threatened with jail time if we made too much noise, the lack of order in the auditorium is refreshing. This place is *rowdy*.

Everybody quiets down when Kirk Watson speaks, though. His eyes narrow as he explains that this is a bill about abortion, so they're talking about *Roe v. Wade*, which is the Supreme Court case that legalized abortion. He says this like he's talking to a very small child, like maybe Nichols is actually a five-year-old who made a wish and got tricked by a genie into an old man's body.

"That's not the body of the bill," Nichols says. "What he's talking about."

"Go to hell!" somebody in the room yells at Evil Santa's giant face on the screen, and people boo again.

Upstairs with Cassie, I felt guilty for thinking that a guy like Nichols is full of crap. Down here, it feels good to be with people who hear something that's clearly a pretense and respond by calling it out. After all, we've already been over this—talking about abortion is germane to the filibuster since the filibuster is about abortion.

But David Dewhurst agrees with Nichols. Cue more booing and hissing. Nichols asks him, "Mr. President, is that a warning?"

"That's the second warning," Dewhurst says, and the room goes *nuts*.

"That's bullshit!" a woman somewhere near the front shouts. Then the roar of the hundreds of people in the auditorium immediately quiets as Wendy Davis appears on the screen.

"Mr. President, I'm not sure that's the second warning," she says, "because it's not a warning to me, the speaker."

Dewhurst looks confused. Then he says to her, "I'm not calling you on a warning. I'm not calling you on a warning. I'm not calling you on a warning," three times in a row like that.

"They really are just making this fucking shit up as they go," I hear a familiar voice say.

I look to my right——Mr. Monaghan is sitting in a chair at the end of a row, next to a lady about his age in an orange shirt. I step over to him.

"Hey!" I say. "This is completely wild, right?"

"Alex?" He seems surprised to see me. "What are you doing here? Why aren't you with Debbie?"

I don't understand the question. I haven't seen Debbie in hours.

"Go downstairs and find her, you asshole," he barks. "She needs help, and you're strong and healthy."

I pull my phone out for the first time in at least an hour, and sure enough, there are a half-dozen texts from Debbie Monaghan, asking me to meet her in E2.002. "Oh, shit. I missed these, I guess."

"Well, get down there," he says. "And when you're done, come back up here. I'll introduce you to Constance. She's my lady friend."

I can't *wait* to meet Constance. I spin away from Mr. Monaghan and stride toward the exit. As I approach the hall, a new senator——a tall, broad-shouldered Black guy——asks questions on the screen.

"If Senator Davis is given three warnings, what impact does that have on her ability to maintain the floor?" he asks.

"Senator West, on the third point of order that

would be sustained, then it's not a warning," David Dewhurst says. "It would be put to the body for a vote."

The Republicans, he's saying, could kill the filibuster.

* * *

I step out of the auditorium and head downstairs to E2.002. Tons of orangeshirts congregate outside of the room, a lot of them eating pizza.

As I walk into the room, I realize how hungry I am. The tables that I set up with those two dudes earlier now have stacks of pizza boxes on them—enormous pizza boxes, like eighteen-inch-pie-sized pizza boxes—but the line has more people than the pizzas will feed. Behind the tables, meanwhile, are two stacks of empty boxes about as tall as a person. Part of me wants to get in line, but then I hear Debbie's voice behind me.

"Alex!" she says. "Thank God you're here. I'm overwhelmed with pizza!"

I start to tell her that it doesn't look like there's much pizza to be overwhelmed by, but then I see a small figure cutting through the swathe of orange people, more or less obscured by the six giant pizza boxes she's carrying. So that's what Shireen has been up to.

Debbie clears a space on one of the tables, and Shireen sets the pizzas down. Then she turns to me.

"You done with *Cassie*, dude?" Shireen says Cassie's name like it's a venereal disease, but I guess she's decided our truce is still on, because she nods her head toward the doors. "There's more."

Okay, I'm on pizza duty.

Debbie shoos us out, and Shireen and I hustle down the hallway, up the stairs, and through the rotunda. Through the windows, I make out a delivery driver—or a delivery driver's car, anyway—just off the street where we dropped off Mr. Monaghan this morning. We pass by the DPS troopers and get to the metal detectors, when Shireen stops, spins on her heel, and puts a hand up in my direction.

"Wait here," she says. "It'll save time if we both don't have to go through security to get back in."

I wait with my hands in my pockets, watching as Shireen hustles along the pavement and picks up the boxes. The state trooper opens the door to let her in. She hands me the pizzas, then turns to go back outside.

"You go take those, then I'll meet you downstairs," she says over her shoulder. "This dude only has a few pizzas left, but he said they have another driver with another dozen coming soon."

I say okay, then turn to head back down the hall.

I navigate my way through the crowded hallway, get to the elevator—the stairs seem impossible to get down while carrying this much pizza—and return to E2.002. The stacks of boxes that were there before are now long gone.

"Have you eaten anything?" Debbie asks as I set my boxes down.

I shake my head, and she gestures to the top box. I grab a slice of mushroom-and-sausage pizza—it's thin crust, the way I like it—and it tastes like heaven. I wolf it down as Shireen appears, a mere three boxes in her hands. She plops them down on another table, then grabs a slice.

"One of the perks of being a runner," she says. "No waiting."

I take a second to look around the room. It's full of people sitting at the tables we brought in, or against the walls, or cross-legged in circles like little kids at recess. Some of them *are* little kids, in fact—there are a lot of parents here with orange-clad children. The space that seemed like a weird classroom earlier today now reminds me of a cross between a medieval feast hall and a refugee camp. Give me your tired, poor, huddled masses as they wear orange T-shirts to show their support for abortion, and I will feed them pizza.

On another table, there are three giant cardboard

catering-style coffee dispensers; underneath the table are four crates of bottled water. Behind that are stacks and stacks of soda cans, and just past the pizzas are boxes and boxes of cookies.

"Wow," I say to nobody in particular. "Where did all of this come from?"

"All over the world," Shireen says. "People asked the pizza place to put notes on the boxes telling us where they came from." She looks at some of the discarded boxes, which have paper receipts stapled to the front. "This one's from Seattle. This one's from Tampa. These three are from Tulsa. This one—cool, this one's from Dublin. This one's from Guatemala!"

"Guatemala?"

"The whole world is watching. The livestream of the filibuster is *everywhere*. There are, like, ten thousand people watching Wendy right now," Shireen says. "And they keep asking Twitter how they can contribute. Debbie started by directing them to the pizza places in town, but after a while we had so much that we started asking for coffee and cookies and water and stuff—just to have some variety. Somebody is supposed to be coming with, like, a giant party sub or three. Everybody wishes they were here right now."

She starts walking toward the door. "Anyway. There's more pizza upstairs. We should go get it."

I follow her out. This time, we walk a little more slowly.

"I can't believe people all over the world care about this," I say. "I mean, this is, like, state senators in Texas. It's not like it's super exciting stuff."

"It's *human rights*," she says with an eye-rolling flourish as we ascend the staircase to the rotunda. "People care about that."

We walk through the hallway and get to the big doors by security. Shireen looks outside, then shakes her head.

"I think we beat 'em here," she says of the pizza delivery drivers.

"Okay," I say. "So explain to me how this became such a big deal. Like, I just found out about it this morning. How did you even start coming here?"

"Well, I came last Thursday. That was the day that all of this started. There was supposed to be, like, a 'citizen's filibuster'——they had a committee meeting where they took testimony, and each person got three minutes," Shireen explains.

I remember Cassie told me about it this morning, though she didn't use phrases like "citizen's filibuster" when she did.

"Anyway, I had my testimony all ready," Shireen says, patting her back pocket. "The list of names was super long, which was amazing. We were basically trying to keep them here all night so they couldn't get on to the next part of the process of passing the bill. It seemed like there were *so many* people there that night, even though there weren't even half as many as there are now."

"And then the guy figured out what the trick was, and he put a stop to it," I say. "I heard about this."

Shireen shakes her head hard and purses her lips. "Who'd you hear that from? Cassie?"

I feel embarrassed again, just thinking about Cassie. I'm not going to get into any of that with Shireen, though, so I don't say anything at all.

"Anyway, that's not how I'd put it," Shireen says. "We were there all night, waiting for our turn—I was waiting for mine, anyway, and there were a few hundred other people there doing the same. And then this guy says that the testimony is getting repetitive, and he's bored of listening to everybody tell their super personal stories about how the state of Texas wants to take away their rights, so he's gonna call it a night. Which, by the way, they've *never* done at one of those things before."

She looks outside again, where a red car with a big metal sign on the roof is pulling up to the curb.

Before she can sprint outside to get the pizza, I ask, "What were you going to testify about?"

Shireen looks at me like I'm a giant dipshit who

just asked her the most ridiculous question in the whole world.

"My abortion," she says, before hustling outside.

6:37 pm

stand there for a minute feeling both stupid —*what a question to ask, Alex, you jerk*— and super curious. I know it must be the worst thing that ever happened to her, but I have to ask. When she comes back—buried under a stack of pizza boxes, her hands shaking and her face clearly upset—I can't help myself.

"Was it Jesse's?" I try to keep my tone gentle and respectful.

"Was *what* Jesse's?" she says like she has no idea what I'm talking about.

"The baby," I say. "The—you know—the abortion."

"Oh." She lets out a disdainful snort-laugh. "Yeah, of course. Dude, your friend who trashed my car is outside. He wants to say hi."

I look past her and finally recognize the red pizza delivery car as a familiar Mustang. Balanced on the hood is another stack of a half-dozen pizza boxes, and leaning against it is Jacob Kohler, with his shaved head, rugby-striped polo shirt, and massive frame, waiting for me. I take a long, deep breath. I would rather do literally anything else on the planet—scrub the floor of a Taco Bell bathroom with my toothbrush, or climb to the top of the rotunda with suction cups on my fingers, or get a tattoo of David Dewhurst's face directly on my forehead—than go out there, but I know that I have to do it, that I can't hide inside here without being the biggest coward in all of Cowardville.

Still, I've been dreading this encounter since the day I went to the police to confess what happened the night we broke Shireen's window.

I didn't *want* to rat out Jacob and Tommy. I wanted to snitch on *myself*. But maybe on the streets that would get me killed? Heck, maybe at the Texas Capitol that'll get me killed. I've watched *The Wire*, and I know what happens to snitches there. I mentally retrace the karate lessons I took for about three months when I was nine—that ought to be good against the ex-star linebacker on our football team, right? I eye the DPS officer who stands at the door—I dub him Officer Friendly and tell myself that if Jacob does decide to beat the hell out of me, he'll probably intervene before I get too beat up.

With that as my pep talk, I open the door and walk outside, directly to the red Mustang that I drove the night Jacob Kohler and Tommy Richman smashed Shireen's window and poured paint all over the cars in Jesse's driveway.

My pulse pounds, and my stomach swoops like I'm on the Rattler wooden rollercoaster at Fiesta Texas and it's just about to take that first massive drop-and-turn combo. The last thing I want to do is talk to Jacob Kohler, but I told Debbie I would get the pizzas, and Jacob Kohler has the pizzas.

"Hey, Collins!" Jacob says as I approach. He gives a big, friendly wave, like an asshole.

I stifle the urge to say "Hey" back. I'm not going to play any more games with this guy. His whole trick is pretending he's your friend before he does something horrible.

For a moment, we stand in silence——me staring, Jacob leaning back against his car with its East Side Pies delivery sign real casual-like.

"So you quit Double Dave's?" I finally squeak.

"I got fired, actually," he says. "The police came while I was at work, believe it or not. Me and Tommy both. Arno fired us that day. You didn't get fired, though, did you?"

I didn't get fired because I quit the day I went to the police so I wouldn't ever have to have this conversation with Jacob.

"I was gonna quit," he continues. "Right before I

went away to Northwestern. But I was gonna work there over the summer, to make some money. You know, beer and poker money for when I was at school. But that all went away when I got arrested, too. I'm taking summer classes at UT now—provisional acceptance. My dad made some calls."

Jacob's dad is a professor at the University of Texas law school, which isn't enough to have kept the police from knocking on his door, but is apparently enough to have gotten him a shot at going to college.

I realize that I don't have any idea what Jacob wants from me. Does he want me to apologize? I don't regret going to the police, but I didn't talk to them to get him in trouble. Does he want me to explain that? I could, but I know he's not much for listening, or nuance.

Finally, I hear a voice say, "I need to pick up those pizzas." It takes me a moment to realize it's *my* voice.

Jacob laughs. "Oh, you want some fucking pizzas? You want me to give you some fucking pizzas?" His voice grows harsher and louder with each word.

Well, now I know what Jacob wants. He wants to beat me up.

I wish I was the sort of person who could narrow his eyes and say, "Why else do you think I'd lower myself to being in your presence?" or something real tough like that, but I'm not. Cassie, with her integrity and passion, would surely say something to stand up for herself. Hell, Shireen—who Jacob hates almost as much as she hates me—actually *did* come out here and get pizzas from him. Both of them are tougher than I am right now. It's all I can do to keep from running back inside.

"Well?" he shouts. "You want some pizzas or what?"

"Yeah," I croak in the most intimidating whisper I can muster.

Jacob marches straight over to me. With two open-palmed hands straight to my chest, he shoves me to the pavement.

I land on my elbows with a thud. When I look up, he has a huge smirk on his face.

"You fell down, Collins," he says.

Officer Friendly isn't paying any attention, and when I try to get up, Jacob shoves me back down. I break my fall with my palms, scraping the hell out of them. I get back to my feet and wipe my face with a bloody palm, then glance around. There are plenty of orange and blue people in the distance, and some of them saw me fall, but this encounter is outside of their world: I'm wearing white, and Jacob is wearing yellow and black.

Jacob laughs as he sees me looking around. "Waiting for another cop to go crying to?"

My elbows and palms are screaming. But I'm fine, I realize. I don't have to fight Jacob Kohler. I just need him to go away.

I stand up, slowly. "I went to the cops to take responsibility for what I did. Why don't you?"

I take a step back when Jacob advances toward me. He's laughing, but I can tell he's furious.

"What the hell are you even talking about?" he bellows. "Who the hell cares about some stupid slut's car and her dead junkie boyfriend's driveway?"

My ears pound with blood. My eyes start to well with tears. I grimace as I choke them down—there's no way in hell I'm going to let Jacob Kohler see me cry. My fingers curl and tense, and my legs pulse with energy. I pull my arm back, preparing to swing, and I catch a big smile on Jacob's face.

And that's when I get it—Jacob is *trying* to get me to hit him. He can get away with a shove, and he can call Shireen and Jesse all the names in the world, but he can't start a fight with me. He's already been in trouble.

I take a big step back.

"You're at work right now," I say. I'm shaking. If I'm wrong, I'm about to get the crap kicked out of me. "And you need to keep this job to stay out of jail." The same thing happened to Bobby when he got busted for possession right before I stopped hanging out at Jesse's house——he had to keep a job as part of his deferred adjudication, or they were going to put him in jail.

"You're such a pussy, Collins," Jacob says. "Like that ugly bitch and your loser friend who OD'd." Now that I know that he's trying to bait me into a fight, he can say whatever horrible things he wants. I don't care what Jacob Kohler thinks of my friends. I never really did.

"I'm not here to talk about them," I say finally, my voice still quivering, but full. "You owe me six pizzas. Or do I need to call that number?" I point to the sign on top of his car.

Jacob glares at me like he wants to kill me, which I'm absolutely certain he does. But he walks back over to the front of his car, picks up the stack of pizzas, and plops them on the pavement.

"You're a piece of shit, Collins," he says as he walks back to the driver's side of his car. "I really hope you know that."

For the first time in months, I feel like that might *not* actually be true.

6:44 pm

'm a mess. My elbows are scraped. My palms are bloody. My shirt's suddenly brown, green, and red from the dirt, grass, and blood. But as I walk through the Capitol with my stack of pizzas, I feel great. After months of feeling like I had something pressing down on me, I feel light. I walk to the beat of "Strange Times," by the Black Keys. I nod my head to imaginary guitar licks. I'm in pain, too—my palms really hurt from falling on them—but who cares? I've been ashamed for the past three months because I was too much of a coward to stand up for myself or do the right thing. Now I've done that, and I survived. I'm even kind of glad, in a weird way, that Jacob Kohler tossed me around. It may not exactly be justice, but it still feels good to have some consequences for the crappy thing I did.

All of that runs through my head as I step around a group of orangeshirts who are loitering in the hall. My heart beats fast. My legs are still all tensed up like they need to run. There's a lot of adrenaline in me, and I don't know what to do with it.

I walk the pizzas down to the subbasement and into E2.002. The room is still crowded, but it's a lot quieter, and there are fewer people in line for food. I realize that everyone is watching the TVs very closely.

I drop the pizza boxes on the table and find Debbie. She's instructing some kids in orange to take empty boxes to a trash can outside while half-watching the television.

"What's going on?" I ask, pointing a thumb to the nearest TV.

"Whoa," she says, wrinkling her nose at me. "What happened to you?"

"I—had an accident," I say, which I guess is kind of true. "It's not important. What's going on in the filibuster?"

"Oh, lord," she sighs. "It's getting silly now. There's another POO"—she pronounces it like "poo," and my face must do something weird, because she explains—"Point of Order. About whether Wendy has her second warning because Senator Ellis helped her adjust her back brace."

"Wait, what? How does that even make sense?"

Debbie throws up her hands like she's been wondering the same thing. "If you have to ask, you're clearly not a member of the Texas GOP Senate delegation."

"So is it not serious, then?" I ask, because that's a pretty calm response.

"Hell, who knows? It probably is. It's bullshit, obviously, but we can't fight the bullshit ourselves. We've got smart people on the floor, and we have to hope that being here to support them is enough." She takes another look at me and my sweaty hair and bloody palms and elbows. "You're off pizza duty till you get cleaned up."

I nod, then go over to one of the TVs to watch what's happening. A Black senator is talking now, passionately arguing a point. I ask the lady closest to me who he is, and she says that he's Senator Ellis.

Ellis is clearly a guy who enjoys telling a good story. He smiles as he goes through his monologue, explaining that he's been a member of the Senate for a very long time, and he's seen really long filibusters before.

"At one point back then, we didn't have the technology that we have today, and he needed to take a break," Ellis says in the same tone my dorky uncle uses when he's about to tell a dirty joke. "But he was so passionate about the issue, whatever it was, at one point he had to take a break and he wouldn't leave the floor, and so the members of the Senate—most of 'em were Democrats back then—stood around his desk. I was in the gallery, but I clearly remember these same wooden trash cans that we have today, and some members of the opposing party were kind enough, dignified enough, and respected this body and its traditions enough to organize his colleagues in both parties to stand around him in a circle, so that he could make the appropriate things that had to be put in place, so he could continue his forty-hour filibuster."

There's laughter in the overflow room—dude just told a story about peeing in a wastebasket on the middle of the Senate floor. Years ago, you could apparently do *that* if you had to, and now Wendy Davis is in trouble over a back brace? Even as Senator Ellis keeps talking, Wendy Davis remains standing—she's been on her feet forever, and she's still on them. No wonder she needs a back brace.

I see Shireen across the room. She looks like she's fuming, staring at the screen with such fiery intensity that David Dewhurst is probably trying to figure out why his face is burning. I wonder what Cassie is thinking right now. She's probably happy, I guess.

I walk over to Shireen and say, "This is pretty wild, huh?"

She shakes her head. "What the hell happened to you?"

I take a deep breath. I need to come clear with Shireen about everything. Taking the consequences with Jacob, even if they were just an awful five minutes and some scrapes and bruises, was the right thing earlier. Taking consequences now by talking to Shireen about what happened that night is right, too. "Look, Shireen, I really need to talk to you about Jacob and the night your car——"

"This is such bullshit," she cuts me off. At first, I think she's talking about me and get confused—— what's bullshit?——but she's back to staring at the TV. "They're seriously——these *men* are seriously going to try to break a filibuster on an abortion bill by telling a woman what she's allowed to do with her body on the floor of the Senate?"

I don't want to get sucked into all of this, so I ask, "Can we go outside for a minute?"

"No," she says, before stepping past me to get closer to the TV, like she really needs a close-up look at Senator Ellis's face.

I'm baffled. She's seriously not going to talk to me?

I step up so I'm next to her again, but she just takes another step forward. I'm trying to make this right——to apologize, even though she's the one who came into my world and messed it up, even though

I'm the one with bloody, burning palms from Jacob Kohler—and she won't even let me talk?

You know your car window is fixed now, anyway, Shireen.

I turn around and storm out of the room.

* * *

I don't look *that* bad, I think, inspecting my reflection in the bathroom mirror. My hair is sweaty and matted, but that could be from sweating in the Senate gallery with Cassie as opposed to spending five minutes in the sun with Jacob. Sure, my shirt is stretched and stained and dirty, but the rest will clean up pretty easy.

I turn on the water and let it run over my hands first. It stings, but only for a minute. I run my wet hands through my hair, to try and get some of the sweat out. Then I squeeze some soap onto my hands and wash my face. I look tired—of course I look tired, it's been a long day—and my eyes are a little sunken and dark.

My shirt's still a mess, but there's not a lot that I can do about that. I still have the blue and orange T-shirts in my bag—but I'm not on anybody's team here.

I don't know what to do with myself, or with Shireen. And now that the adrenaline has worn off from my encounter with Jacob, I realize I might not have seen the end of him, either. If I had a car, I reckon there's a good chance it'd end up with a brick through the back window tonight.

What I really need to do is talk to Shireen, to get that whole thing out in the open. She needs to hear from me that I was there the night her window got smashed, and she needs to know how bad I feel about it. She also needs to know that I have a right to be upset with her, that what started happening at Jesse's house ruined my life.

But I don't know how to have that conversation with her if she keeps running away from me when I try to bring it up. She saw Jacob out there, and she saw me afterward—she had to have figured out that we're not still friends. It's all confusing, and I don't know what to do—and then it occurs to me that the most decent person I know is up in the Senate gallery, wearing a blue dress and watching Wendy Davis. I know she thinks I'm a jerk right now, but we talked about some really intense stuff, and I don't think she's the type of person to blow that off. So I rinse my face, dry off, and head upstairs to find Cassie.

But the line for the Senate gallery is out of control and longer than ever. Of course it would be—it's been over an hour since I left, and in that hour, a whole bunch of people got off work, parked, walked over to the Capitol, and started waiting in line to watch in person.

I keep going up the stairs, though, just to make sure that this really is the right line and that it goes all the way to the Senate gallery door, just in case they abruptly opened an Apple Store in the Capitol and this is actually a line full of people waiting for the new iPhone and they're all wearing orange by coincidence.

About midway through the second floor—maybe fifty people away from the entrance—I see a familiar face: Mr. Monaghan, who's standing beside a woman who must his lady friend Constance. Mr. Monaghan hasn't noticed me, but I'm not sure if that's because his vision is bad or because his eyes are focused elsewhere.

"Hey, Mr. Monaghan," I say, and he looks at me, his eyes flashing with recognition.

"Alex!" he kinda shouts, then his eyes adjust to the sight of me. "Jesus, kid, what happened to you? You look like shit. And call me Sean."

"Sorry," I say. I stick my hand out to introduce myself to Constance. "Hi. My name's Alex."

Constance wears dark tinted glasses and an orange shawl over her blouse. Her hair is gray and cut short and stylish. She shakes my hand warmly. "Oh, you're the boy Sean reads with. It's nice to meet you. He speaks very highly of you—and your accents."

"I'll spare you," I say. "How do you two know each other?"

"Old drinking buddies," Mr. Monaghan says. "Connie's a Rangers fan, but I never held it against her too much. This place is like a reunion. I saw my old dentist on the elevator, and Connie and a few other old birds—"

Constance slaps him playfully.

Mr. Monaghan chuckles. "Anyway, lots of people here. And you—what are you doing here? Did you get one of the orange shirts from Debbie? Where's your little friend, the short girl?"

I could fill him in—I don't know; it's in my bag; she's downstairs being completely impossible—but I feel silly talking about that stuff in front of Constance and everybody else in line, so instead I scratch at the back of my neck and ask, "Do you have a minute? I could use some advice."

I'd rather talk to Cassie, but if I can't get in to see her, I'll settle for the foul-mouthed octogenarian who cried, "The fucking prick finally did it!" when Joffrey had Ned Stark beheaded.

Mr. Monaghan gestures with his hand, like "go ahead." As he does, the Senate gallery door opens to let a few people out. A woman by the door shouts,

"We love you, Wendy!" and the rest of the line quickly takes it up as a chant.

"We looove you / Wen-dy! We looove you / Wen-dy!" suddenly roars through the room. The state trooper manning the door shuts it quickly, which just inspires the chanting to get louder.

Mr. Monaghan sighs. I nod my head toward a hall-way that I remember from field trips leads to offices.

"I'll be back in a minute," he says to Constance, and the two of us walk down the hallway while she holds his place.

The hall isn't crowded, but there are still some scattered people in blue and orange checking their tweets or whatever. You can still hear "We looove you / Wen-dy!" louder than you can hear the person standing next to you, so I lead Mr. Monaghan to an office door. It's unlocked, so I go inside, and Mr. Monaghan follows.

"Everything all right?" he asks. "You're acting fucking squirrelly."

"I don't know what to do about Shireen," I say.

"Are you in love with her? Just tell her. You came all the way down here to be with her, so she probably already knows. Women are smart about that stuff. We always think it's some big fucking secret, and they already know. She's probably had boys sniffing around since she was thirteen, so she knows what that looks like by now," he says, shaking his head. "Just tell her."

"She's not the girl I came down here for," I tell him. "Shireen——we used to be friends, a long time ago. But we had a falling out, and now she won't listen to me. But I need her to do that. I need to—— honestly, I need to *apologize* to her, and she won't let me! You don't know her. If you did——" I laugh, thinking about Mr. Monaghan and how *he'd* put it if he had this problem. "If *you* knew her, you'd probably call her a total fucking bitch."

Mr. Monaghan does not laugh. Instead, he looks at me through narrowed eyes, shakes his head in disgust, and spits on the carpeted floor of Texas State Rep. Whoever's small office.

"Is that what you think I'd say?" His voice is thick with disappointment.

"I mean——" I'm not sure what's happening here. "Just, like, because you swear a lot?" My voice trails off.

"Jesus fucking Christ, Alex," he says. "I like you. You're a good kid. I know you have to come down and read to me, and I know you're lonely, but you make an effort, and I appreciate that. I'm grateful for the company, and you're a hell of a lot better than the church kids who come in. But if you think I'm the sort of man who'd call a woman a fucking bitch, then clearly you don't know a fucking thing about me."

I'm so confused. "But you say stuff like that all the time . . . ?"

"Fuck that," he says. He seems really angry, like I managed to both disappoint and offend him. "I never called a woman a bitch in my fucking life. I'm gonna tell you something, kid, because I like you, I do. You're a sweetheart, even if you sound like a fucking asshole right now. So I'm going to explain it to you. There are two kinds of men in the world: the kind who think that women deserve a whole separate class of insult to put them in their place, and the kind who think that guys who *do* believe that shit are pieces of fucking garbage. And you get to pick which kind of man you are. But if you're the kind who thinks that you need the word *bitch* to put down a girl who pisses you off, then a guy like me is always going to be there watching, and we'll always know what you *really* are."

Don't cry. Don't cry. Don't cry. I know my face is bright red right now. Mr. Monaghan stares at me through those narrow eyes, like he's trying to size me up. *Don't cry.* But man, I really want to. Is that what he thinks? That I'm a piece of fucking garbage?

I take a deep breath in. Jacob Kohler calls girls bitches all the time. If the two options for the kind of man I can be are Mr. Monaghan and Jacob, it's an easy decision. I let the air out of my lungs slowly, and I don't want to cry anymore.

"Okay," I say. "You wouldn't call her that, and neither would I." Mr. Monaghan nods, like this is a test that I just passed. "But I still don't know what to do."

"Well, let me ask you a question," he says. His voice is much gentler now, and he clasps my shoulder like we just shared some tough love and need to hug it out. "Have you been treating her like you think she's 'a fucking bitch'?" His voice rises, like he's trying to sound like a teenager.

I'm getting pretty tired of seeing myself through Mr. Monaghan's eyes, but hoo boy, I thought I should have consequences for the crappy things I've done, and I am getting what I asked for. I nod just a fraction of an inch. "Maybe," I admit.

"Well, there's your fuckin' problem," he says. Then he sits down in one of the desk chairs, like he's just exhausted by me. "Look, Alex. You really are a good kid, but you got a lot of asshole in you. It's not your fault—that's just part of being a kid. I was a hundred times worse when I was your age, for goddamn sure. But the short girl—she doesn't know if she's gonna get the asshole or the good kid. You want to apologize to her, you gotta find a way to let her know that she's not gonna be hearing from the asshole."

I plop down in another chair, exhausted by myself. "But how can I do that if she won't even let me talk about it?"

"If she doesn't want to talk about it, and you keep pushing her, then you're showing her the asshole," he says like it's the most obvious thing in the world. "Listen to what she's telling you. If you want to apologize and she doesn't want to hear it, who are you doing it for? Her? Or you?"

I barely even understand the question, but this sounds like another one of those "two types of people in the world" deals. I guess I *do* want to apologize to make myself feel better. If she doesn't want to hear it, that's up to her, though, not me.

"You're here, she's here, there's a hell of a lot of shit happening out there"—Mr. Monaghan gestures to the world outside of this office we snuck into—"and she probably needs some fucking help with all of it right now. All of this shit is a lot more personal to somebody who can get pregnant than it is to me or you, I'll tell you that for fucking free. So go out there and be the good kid you are, not the asshole you feel like being, and help her out."

I remember what Shireen told me right before she went outside to pick up the pizzas from Jacob—that her testimony was about her own abortion, which I never even knew she had. It seems wild to me that she would tell *me* about it, knowing that she thinks I'm just the ex-friend jerk who broke her window. But she *did* open up to me about it, and she probably did that for some reason.

I nod at Mr. Monaghan and stand. "Okay. That makes a lot of sense."

"Oh, and Alex?" he says as he gets up. "You really should tell her you love her."

7:31 pm

When we leave the office, the "We looove you / Wen-dy!" chants have died out, and the entire space feels different. Even though it's almost all orangeshirts out here, the atmosphere is decidedly tense. People are staring intently at their phones or talking in frustrated, hushed tones.

When we get back to Constance, the people in line behind her step aside to let Mr. Monaghan back where he had been—but they eye me suspiciously.

"You were here earlier, of course, sir," a young woman in orange says to Mr. Monaghan. Then she gestures to me. "But I don't want to lose my spot if your friend goes in, too."

"I'm not in line," I say. "I'm just keeping them company."

She nods and smiles. "Okay, then."

She seems firm but friendly, like a lot of women here, actually. Like Shireen and Debbie and Constance, at least, she's happy to talk to me so long as I don't push boundaries. She's got a round face and dark hair—I'd guess she's Latina—and she's short, but not, like, Shireen-short.

"So what's going on in there?" I ask her. "Everything out here seems pretty tense."

"They sustained the second POO"—she pronounces it "poo," too—"a few minutes ago. The back-brace thing. Apparently, a filibuster is an 'endurance contest,' and if somebody helps you so you don't fall over, then you're doing it wrong."

"But that other guy said they used to let people pee in the garbage cans, didn't he?"

She shrugs real big, like the ¯_(ツ)_/¯ emoji guy. "She's just lucky she's got a diaper on today. They're not really concerned with being consistent here, I don't think."

She has to wear a *diaper*? Good grief. But I gloss over that, since everyone else seems to think it's normal, and remember what Shireen said earlier, about the men on the floor punishing a female senator for doing the wrong thing with her body. It's actually a really smart point, I decide, so I go ahead and repeat it. "So you've got a bunch of men on the Senate floor telling a woman what she is and isn't allowed to do with her body?"

"Yes! Exactly! Thank you. And they're trying to basically end abortion for thousands and thousands of Texas women because she had somebody help her put a back brace on. You get it," she says with what sounds like admiration.

I flush, embarrassed to be told how awesome I am just because I repeated something smart that Shireen said an hour ago.

"Anyway," the woman goes on, "I just think about all of those women, and how they're going to suffer because these people are determined to shut Wendy down however they can."

And transgender men, I think, remembering what Shireen said earlier today. And me, I guess, if I ever get somebody pregnant and she needs to get an abortion.

But I just say, "Yeah. There are a lot of people in Texas who don't want this to pass."

"Not just in Texas," she says. "I drove in from Norman, Oklahoma, this morning. The closest abortion clinic to my parents' house is in Dallas. There are people from Louisiana here, and Arkansas, too, I'm sure. We all need this to work. But they can't help her put on a friggin' back brace."

I didn't think about the fact that people in other states might rely on Texas's clinics, too, and I find myself wanting to tell Shireen about it.

"That's messed up," I agree. Then I say my goodbyes so I can head downstairs to look for Shireen.

As I walk back along the line, things still feel very tense, like everybody is having the exact same head-ache at the exact same time. People shake their heads as they stare at their phones, presumably following the action. I pull my phone out, but I don't even know where to find out what's happening. I go to Twitter and see that #StandWithWendy is trending, so I click that. The first tweet is from @BarackObama, who says, "Something special is happening in Austin tonight" with a link to a livestream of the filibuster. So the president is watching this? Wow.

He's not the only one, though—as I scroll down, I can see that there are more than fifty thousand people watching the livestream now, which is just insane to me. That's half as many people as fit into the UT football stadium. There are pictures going around of Wendy Davis with Khaleesi's dragons from *Game of Thrones* photoshopped onto her shoulder.

Finally, I get the gist of what's happening inside: After the second POO, Wendy Davis and the other Democrats in the Senate got really nervous. It's three-strikes-and-you're-out, and when strike two is already across the plate, you don't want to take a wild swing. So, she's just reading a long policy paper written in legalese that I can barely make any sense of. I close the app, put my phone back in my pocket, and give up figuring out exactly what I think of anything.

Back in E2.002, there are still cookies, pizzas, sodas, water bottles, salads, and coffee dispensers that people from Chile or Egypt or Norway or wherever sent to keep the orangeshirts fed and caffeinated and refreshed, but the room is less crowded now. I'm guessing most people are full and have gone to the auditorium to watch and cheer or boo at the big screen. But Debbie is still here, standing behind one of the tables and instructing orange-shirted teenagers to grab pizza boxes and make for the trash.

"Do you need help with anything?" I ask her. "I'm a little bit cleaner."

"I think we've got it for now, but stay close," she says. "We're in a lull right now, but new people keep showing up, and the donations keep coming."

I nod and glance over to one of the televisions. Standing next to the wall, shifting her weight, and chewing one of her black-polished nails is Shireen, her dark curls over her eyes as she appears to be both avoiding the TV and simultaneously desperate to keep an eye on it.

I walk over, determined to keep what Mr. Monaghan said in mind and to not push her on anything. I *want* to apologize; she doesn't *owe me* the chance to do that.

"How long has she been reading?" I ask.

"Forever," Shireen says. "I wish, anyway. I hope

she just reads this whatever-it-is for the next four hours until it's time to go home."

I listen to Wendy Davis speak for a moment. She's still reading from something about "fetal pain." It's boring, but the idea that an abortion hurts the baby—like, physically makes it suffer—is one that I've been thinking about since I talked to Cassie earlier today. I don't know when it stops being a fetus and starts being a baby, but I figure if it can feel pain, then it's probably a person. Wendy Davis, meanwhile, reads from what sounds like a medical journal about how there's no evidence that fetuses *do* feel pain. It'd be convincing, I guess, but what if they're wrong? How can anybody actually know?

"What do you think about all of this?" I ask Shireen.

"It's total bullshit," she says. "I mean, good for her for sticking with it, but she's being so careful now. One of the white guy senator dudes—one of the Republicans, I mean—tried to interrupt her to ask questions, and she just shook her head and kept going."

"No," I say. "I mean, what do you think about what she's reading? About when the baby can feel pain?"

"How the hell am I supposed to know?" she asks.

I don't know what to say, so I just stand next to

her, listen some more, and wish that I knew what I thought about this. I think about Cassie and her conviction, and what that means to her—everything from calling me this morning to standing in line to get into the Senate gallery to staying up there without anything to eat or drink or the chance to go to the bathroom—and I don't just *admire* her for it, I'm *jealous* of her for it.

There are fifty thousand people watching this on the internet right now, and thousands more who came down here in person, some from out of state. People worldwide are spending their money just to make sure that Debbie Monaghan and Shireen Dehghan have something to eat while they're here, because they don't want anybody to have to leave. The entire world is watching because this is so important.

The buses of blueshirts and the hordes of orangeshirts and those weird, aloof dudes who helped me set up E2.002—all of them know that this is the most important place they could be right now. And those fifty thousand people watching on the internet—including, I guess, Barack Obama—I bet a bunch of them would be down here showing their support in person if they could.

And here I am, still not knowing what I believe.

Outside, there's probably a group of people in blue led by Father Mosier who are chanting "It's a child, not a choice!" while on the other side of the Capitol, there are probably a zillion people in orange chanting "Her body, her choice!" And I'm here in my white T-shirt because I don't know which side I should join. Is it a child or is it a choice? Which side is right?

So finally, I turn to Shireen. "Can I ask you a question?"

She sighs a little, like she's ready to bounce if the question is something she doesn't want to answer. "Sure."

"What are you doing here?" I ask. "I mean, I know why you're here—like, I know you want the filibuster to work. But what made you decide to come down here in the first place?"

"I came on Thursday because I wanted to tell my story during testimony," she says. "I'm not naive enough to think that telling my story would change anybody's mind, but I wanted to do my part in the citizen's filibuster to help stop the bill. Then, when they shut down the meeting and kicked us out, I started coming back for a few reasons, I guess."

She keeps her eyes fixed on the TV as she shakes her head a little. She looks really sad, and I want to, like, put a hand on her shoulder or something. I think again about the fact that she had an abortion—and that the baby would have been Jesse's—and I can only imagine how guilty she must feel about that now. I realize how lucky I am that I don't have to make that sort of decision.

"What were the reasons?" I ask.

"Well, partly because I like all of these people. I like Debbie——she found me that first night and drafted me into setting up tables for pizzas, and I wanted to feel useful because I'd felt so useless just standing there watching them shut us out. But also, I just wanted to witness it. I wanted them to know that they couldn't sneak this through——that if they were going to do this, they were going to do it while I was staring at them. They'd have to see me standing there while they took away my rights."

"Yeah," I say. "I get that. Cassie said pretty much the same thing this morning, about why she's here—— she wanted Wendy Davis to have to see her, too. It's like, they're not *bad people*, but they need to think about——"

"Oh, they're bad people," Shireen says with a bitter laugh. "All these little games they're playing—— giving her a second strike because someone helped her with a back brace? Giving her the first strike be-cause she talked about fucking Planned Parenthood, because apparently one of the main organizations that performs abortions isn't relevant to a bill about abortion? All of the times they keep interrupting her to trick her into yielding? The fact that they kicked us out on Thursday in the first place! They're bad people. They're not listening to us at all. We're *right here*, and they're not listening to us. They're doing everything they can to stop listening. I mean, literally to stop *listening.* They're trying every dirty trick they have, basically cheating, just so they don't have to *listen.* That's what it's about, dude. It's about listening to us. And they don't want to."

Shireen looks at me like she expects me to argue or ask a question, but I don't. I just nod. This part of it, I do feel like I understand.

"So anyway," Shireen continues, "I came back over the weekend, just so they'd see me. And I'm here today because I want Wendy to know that I'm here. I want her to know what it means to me that *she's* here. I didn't get to tell my story—those assholes took that from me—but she's standing there, all day and all night, with her back brace, and she must have to pee *so bad,* and I'm sure she's tired and hungry and her feet hurt and all the rest. She's out there so she can tell my story—everybody's story—for us." Shireen turns toward the screen, where Wendy Davis talks about something-or-other, but she's not sad this time. She's got a hint of a smile on her face.

"Right," I say after a second. "She's doing it now

because you can't. Your voices don't matter anymore, but hers still does."

Shireen nods, her smile fading fast. "Yeah," she admits. "It sucks to realize that you don't have any power over your own life—your own body. I wish my voice mattered. But if it doesn't, then I'll be here for her, to let her speak for me."

I do put my hand on Shireen's shoulder then, just for half a second. I feel embarrassed, like what the hell am I doing? After all, we're still enemies, kind of. But she doesn't seem to mind. She just exhales, sharply, through her nose.

"Anyway," she says after I've moved my hand away. "What the hell happened to you outside, dude? You look like hell."

"I thought I cleaned up okay," I say, and she snort-laughs.

"Yeah, except for that disgusting T-shirt and whatever happened to the rest of you." She waves her hands at me.

"Jacob Kohler happened to me," I say after a moment. Part of me doesn't want to press this into unfriendly territory now that we're getting along better, but the other part of me really, really does, if only so we can have it out.

"I thought you guys were buddies," she says, with a mix of surprise and bitterness.

"No," I say quietly. "Not anymore."

She's quiet for a minute. "Yeah," she says finally. "I kind of guessed that."

"You did?" I ask.

"I mean, you *did* come back in looking pretty messed up," she says, a faint trace of a smile on her lips.

"Yeah, we haven't been friends in a while. Honestly, I don't think we were ever friends," I say, my voice a little distant. I know she doesn't want to hear my apology, but she did ask what happened. So I just talk. "He's just one of those people who need to have, like, a group of followers listening to him, and I was one of them, for a little while. But not—not since—you know—not since that night. Outside of Jesse's house. I know—I know that you know what happened. I mean—I think you know. Right?"

"When you drove those guys over to your best friend's house so they could throw a brick through my window?"

My face burns. "Right," I say. "That."

Now that we're talking, I realize that it's okay to apologize. This is what Mr. Monaghan was talking about earlier: If I'm pushing the topic when I know that she doesn't want me to, then I'm the one who's being a jerk. If she *does* want to talk about it, though, then it's different. So I come out with it.

"I really am sorry," I say. "I am *so* sorry. I didn't know where we were going that night or why. If I'd known—I mean, I was mad at you, and at Jesse, and at everybody else over there—but I wouldn't have gone over there to mess you up."

"I know," she says with a small nod. "That's why you called Jesse's mom and went to the police."

Wait, *what*?

The room spins.

"Well, yeah," I say, suddenly indignant. "I—I didn't know you knew *that* part."

"Yeah, Jesse's mom told us. Not everybody—just me and Jesse. I saw Jacob's car take off after the alarm, and I knew that you had been hanging out with those guys a lot, so I figured you were in on it. But when we talked to Jesse's mom in the morning, she told us that you didn't know what they were planning and that you confessed to it right away."

"So wait," I say, my voice rising. "You *knew*? You knew that I didn't know where we were going that night, and you knew that I tried to make it right the very next day, and you've still been treating me like I'm the biggest jerk in the great state of Texas? How much does a new window even cost, Shireen? Do you need me to pay you back? I quit my job, but I still have a little bit saved up—"

"You *are* the biggest jerk in the great state of

Texas," Shireen says, staring at me with eyes like little daggers. She breathes hard out her nose. "I was never mad at you about the stupid window, Alex."

"Then why? I know why *I've* been mad at *you* for the past six months, but I have no earthly idea why you've been treating me like I'm history's greatest monster if it's not about your car."

"Because you *left him*, Alex," she hisses. "Right when he needed you to be there—when *I* needed you to be there—you left. And things got so much worse when you did."

I don't even know what she's talking about. If anybody in that group needed me, they never let me know about it. All they did was make me feel like I had no reason to be there in the first place. And whose fault was that again?

"Well, then," I say, my voice full of the same spite and anger she sent my way moments earlier, "I guess you shouldn't have brought the beer and the weed and the—whatever else he was doing before he died—into his life."

Shireen looks at me like I just spoke in Polish.

"I didn't bring anything into his life, dude," she says, gently. "That was all Bobby."

8:29 pm

Room E2.002 in the Texas State Capitol extension is a very confusing place to be all of a sudden.

"But I saw you," I say. I should be furious—she's lying to me, I know she's lying to me because I *saw* her. But she's looking at me sympathetically, like she feels sorry for me, and my anger melts to uncertainty. "You brought weed over. Your sister brought the beer. I was there, Shireen. The first time he tried it. You were the one who started it all."

Shireen shakes her head. "I picked it up for him a few times, yeah," she says. "I was trying to fit in, too. And when we first started smoking weed together, it was fun. When it was just a little weed, or just getting drunk and being silly and all of that—at first, it was fun. But I didn't get anybody started on that. That was Bobby. Jesse and Bobby had been getting messed up together for months before I did any of that with them. I assumed that you were doing it, too. You guys all did everything together."

I stand there in E2.002, trying to recall those days. Whenever I've thought about it, I've pictured the big roving party all hanging out, but this time, I think about going into the garage apartment right after school and seeing Jesse and Bobby on the couch, drinking beers while I killed time before work. Bobby was a big, goofy guy, and he was there all the time. I didn't mind—he always lightened the mood, and his house was such a nightmare that I didn't blame him for not wanting to be there. But we also didn't really hang out, just me and him. Maybe Bobby was *Jesse's* friend, not mine?

"But you were—you had to have known that it was getting bad over there," I stammer. "And—and you helped make it worse." I don't even know what I'm saying now—I just want to keep blaming Shireen for something. Why is it so important to me that this is her fault?

"Listen, dude," she says. "I knew it was getting way too intense over there. I mean, I had fun with it every once in a while, especially when it was just weed. And if it had only been every once in a while, it would have been fine. But Jesse—Jesse got into it *hard.* You saw that."

I feel those tears again, and I'm so pissed that they're in my eyes, but there are tears threatening to mess up Shireen's impeccable eyeliner and mascara, too, so I just let mine build. "Yeah, I saw that," I say.

"I mean, for me, that stuff never meant much. I could do it or not do it, it didn't matter," Shireen says. She sounds like she's in confessional, like she's not exactly explaining it to *me* so much as she's just *saying* it. Maybe with everything that's happened in the past few months she hasn't had anybody that she could say any of this to?

"But Jesse loved getting messed up so much that it started to scare me. And I couldn't be the only good influence on him. I couldn't try to pull him out of it on my own. His mom——I mean, you know that his mom liked to put her head in the sand. And you weren't there anymore. You left when it was still mostly just beer and weed, but it got so much worse after that. I think because Jesse looked up to you so much, and he knew that you had all that history with your dad——I don't think he wanted you to see him like that."

Jesse looked up to *me*? That doesn't make any sense. He was the center of that universe——he was the one people came to see, the one with the party space and the cute girlfriend, the one the older kid from down the block liked to hang out with. He was Jon Snow; I was Samwell Tarly.

"Well, I didn't *want* to see him like that," I say,

choking my words out. After all the times I've wanted to cry today—when Jacob talked about Jesse, when Mr. Monaghan laid into me—it finally happens now.

"I didn't, either. But I couldn't help him." Shireen's crying now, too, big tears. I realize the forty or fifty other people in this room with us are staring.

Suddenly, Shireen grabs my hand and leads me out of the room and down the hall. We walk past people in orange, but nobody stops us—two crying teenagers isn't the weirdest thing anybody's seen here today. I try the doors of a few offices, but they're locked. Finally, we go to the end of the dark hall and sit down on the floor.

I'm a little calmer now. Just moving around helps, sometimes, when the despair about Jesse hits. It's probably why I've been riding my bike so much lately.

We sit quietly for a few minutes, then Shireen looks over at me. She reaches into her back jeans pocket and pulls out a piece of printer paper. She unfolds it and refolds it a few times. I don't press her about what it says. I just sit there with her because she's the only person I know who might understand what it feels like to be thinking of Jesse right now.

"I never got to read my testimony on Thursday night," she finally says. "Wendy Davis read a lot of people's testimony this afternoon, but she didn't get to mine. Which is fine—she must have had hundreds to choose from. But it means nobody got to hear it. You asked me why I keep coming down here, and all the things I told you are true—but also, I've been coming down here because I want somebody to hear what I have to say."

I keep my mouth shut and nod.

"It's funny," she says. "I've always been told that I can write well. By teachers and stuff. I'm not sure what I want to be when I'm older, or what I want to study in college. But last year, Mrs. Campbelton told me I should be a writer. She said, 'I really hope you keep doing this,' when she handed back my term paper at the end of the year. 'You have a gift.' Which was awesome to hear. Who doesn't like gifts, right?

"But when I sat down to write this, I realized that I don't have whatever gift she thought I did. Because I started this and deleted it and wrote half a page and deleted it and finished a version and deleted it a million times last Thursday."

"What about that one?" I ask gently, gesturing to the paper in her hands. "Would you throw that one out and start over again, too, if you could?"

She thinks about it for a minute, then shakes her head. Her curls bounce when she does. "Nah," she says. "It doesn't have to be perfect. It just has to be true."

"Can I hear it?" I ask.

She nods and unfolds the paper one more time.

"Hello," she starts, reading aloud from the page like she would have done on Thursday night, if they had let her. "My name is Shireen Dehghan. I'm here today as a concerned Texas resident, opposing the bills being considered by the legislature today.

"I want to tell you my story, even though I'm sure this is the sort of story that so many people dread. It's a story about someone who decided to have an abortion because she didn't want to have a baby. I know it's easier when it's a story about somebody who was raped, or somebody whose life was in danger. If enough people show up today, you'll probably hear those stories, too. But this is my story. It's not as tragic as those—it just ends the same way. It ends with somebody making the right decision for herself.

"I got pregnant when I was seventeen. I'm still seventeen now, but that's how old I was then, too. I don't know how it happened—I've been on birth control since I started having my period, but I guess I might have missed a dose. I didn't think I was all that irresponsible. My boyfriend and I had only started having sex a few months earlier. We usually used condoms, but we were both virgins when we started, and we wanted to see how it felt. There were a lot of things we wanted to experience together.

"One thing we didn't want to experience was what

it was like to become parents. Or, at least, I didn't want to experience that with him. I don't know if he wanted to experience it with me because I never told him."

Whoa. Jesse didn't even *know*? I open my mouth to ask her about that, but then I think about what Mr. Monaghan said and turn my head. I'm not going to interrupt her. I try not to even make eye contact, so she can just keep going without having to wonder what I'm thinking.

"I'm telling you my story right now, and I know that some of you are judging me. I know that some of you think I'm a slut for having sex, that I'm a murderer for having an abortion, that I'm selfish because I didn't tell my boyfriend about it first. I'm telling you my story because every time we talk about this topic, we talk about the girl who got pregnant when her brother raped her or the woman who died because she couldn't get an abortion. I care about those people—but I also care about me. And when you debate how many weeks is too many weeks, or how wide the clinic's hallways have to be, or if my doctor has to be registered at a hospital in addition to the clinic, you're forgetting about me.

"I want you to know that all the questions you have about abortion—whether a fetus can feel pain, or whether I should have just kept my legs shut if

I didn't want a baby, or whether life begins at con-ception—all of those are questions you're allowed to have. But while you're debating philosophical ques-tions, I'm making decisions about the rest of my life. And even people who aren't perfect have a right to make those decisions. That's why I'm here today opposing these bills. Thank you for your time."

I take a minute before I look up at Shireen, who does look nervous. I don't know what to do—part of me wants to, like, applaud or give her a hug or tell her I'm sorry that it ever happened to her. It's so weird that I knew her when she was pregnant—that I was there, even if I didn't know it was happening.

"So that's what I was hoping to say," she says. "I'm glad somebody got to hear it."

I think I understand what she means, why she's so passionate about abortion as a right that she was willing to say all of that in front of a bunch of old white men. But for just a second, I think back to Cassie and the other side of the argument. Because we're talking softly here in this hallway, it feels okay to ask her the question I've been struggling with this whole day.

"That all makes sense, but I've heard a lot of stuff that sounded like it made sense on the other side, too," I say. I'm doing my best to sound nice.

"Is there ever a situation where you think a person *shouldn't* get an abortion?"

Shireen looks at me like she doesn't understand the question, then finally squints and answers. "Um, sure? If they don't want one?"

It's a simple answer, but it hits me right in the chest. Cassie is here because Cassie's mom decided not to have an abortion—not because it was illegal to do that.

Now that we're being real with each other, I can't stop myself from blurting out the other question on my mind. "Do you regret it now? I mean, because it was Jesse's?"

Shireen shakes her head softly and looks at me with her eyes big and sympathetic. Her lips are pursed into a tight smile, like she feels bad for me for missing something so glaringly obvious. "No," she says. "Dude, no."

"But you could have—you could have, like, had a piece of him forever."

"I know," she says. "And I've thought about it. I even have dreams about it sometimes. But I always wake up relieved, and then I go back to working on college applications. I think about Jesse every day. I miss him every day. I loved him. But this is my life, and my body. I wouldn't turn that into a memorial for him, just because of what happened."

"What about adoption?" I ask. "You could have had the baby and then given it up for adoption."

Shireen nods. "Yeah, I thought about that, too. But then I asked myself, why? Because I don't think abortion is wrong. I don't think I need to give up control over my own body if I don't want to. I'm not an incubator."

"Do you wish you had told Jesse?"

She exhales slowly, like that's a harder question. "It wouldn't have changed anything. It probably would have made him feel guilty, like it was his fault. Even though it was just something that happened. When I got the abortion, I knew it was for both of us—he certainly couldn't have been a dad. Jesus. But he wasn't in a place where he could hear that. Not at that point. I wish that he could have, though," she says softly. After a moment, she adds, "I didn't tell anybody except for my mom. And I was terrified to tell her, but you have to, in Texas, if you're a minor—which sucks, by the way. And telling her that I needed an abortion seemed less scary than telling her that I was going to have a baby. But, you know, my family is from Iran. My parents are way more traditional than most of my friends' parents. She didn't tell my dad, but she understood that I needed an abortion when I told her. She told me that she was glad that we were here, where it was relatively easy to get one. She said that when she was my age, she saw girls have to find their own ways to do it. So I was glad that I told her, even though it was really difficult. But Jesse—I couldn't tell Jesse. I just couldn't imagine that conversation. By that point, Jesse wasn't even Jesse anymore."

It's true, I think. *It's absolutely true.* There were flashes of him—every once in a while, there were flashes where I could see him still, where it felt like we were still the same kind of friends we had been. They were rare, but they happened. I didn't know anybody else felt that way. How did Shireen even stand it?

"I know," I say. "I mean, I know that feeling really well. That's why—when I had to go, I had to go, and I couldn't come back. That's the thing that was so hard for me." My voice rises. "I know you were mad at me—I know you *are* mad—because I wasn't there when he needed me to be. But there wasn't even a *him* to be there for so much of the time. And that was the hardest part. It wasn't the constant party or the jerky new friends—it was that he was *gone.*"

Shireen unfurls her legs out from under her, leans her head forward, and looks down. "I wanted to find a way to get him to come back so bad," she says, her voice thick and tight. "And I couldn't do it. Not by myself. No matter what I did, I couldn't get him to come back. I decided I was going to tell his mom, but I kept putting it off. I thought about breaking up with him so much. If I hadn't been so scared for him, I would have. But all of his other friends—Bobby and Holly and everybody else, even the people who were my friends first—they weren't there to help, they just made it worse. If you had been there, I don't know if you could have saved him. But I know that if you had been there, at least I wouldn't have been alone in trying."

I look at her, this girl I've hated for so long because I thought she was the cause of a problem that she only ever tried to fix, and she stares at me, this boy she's hated for so long because he left her alone with something too big for any of us. Her cheeks are wet with tears and dark with smeared mascara, and I feel a tightness in my throat that I know means I'm not done crying today. I swallow it down, though, because I don't want to cry right now. I need to get this out.

"Jesse was my best friend," I say. "I was so mad at him and at you and at everybody else, too. Because you—all of you—you were the best thing in my life. I loved you. I loved him. You don't know what it was like for me before I met him. And then I couldn't stay, because there was nothing there for me anymore. It was all dark and scary and awful, and I realized that I didn't matter anymore. He was my best friend, Shireen"—and god, the tears are welling back up. "I'd have followed him anywhere—except for the place that he was going. I couldn't do that."

I lose it again, thinking about those days and about Jesse, my dead friend, and how I didn't go to the funeral because I felt too guilty—for the night with the brick and the paint, yeah, but mostly for leaving at all, because it's not like Shireen is saying anything I didn't already know. It's not like I haven't thought a million times every day since the day he died that if I hadn't left, maybe somehow he would still be here.

Shireen pulls me close, and we cry in each other's arms after saying these things out loud to someone else for the first time. We sit there, my enemy and I, both of us thinking about this boy we loved in different ways, who died because we couldn't save him.

8:51 pm

After what feels like forever, Shireen and I let go of each other. We're not crying anymore. I don't know how Shireen feels right now, but it's probably like how I feel: sad, and tired, and relieved that somebody else gets it. I offer her my hand to get up, and she grabs it. She wipes a finger under her eye, and it comes back thick with mascara.

"I should find a bathroom," she says, then laughs a kind of awkward, brittle laugh as we attempt to rejoin society.

We walk down the hall, and she doesn't seem to mind that anybody who turns her direction can see the smeared makeup on her face, because of course Shireen's fearlessness extends to not caring if people can tell that she's been crying.

The bathroom is surrounded by a bunch of orangeshirts who are eating pizza—apparently a new wave of hungry people showed up—or talking, or tweeting, or reading tweets, or whatever it is people are doing on their phones. I take my phone out, because what else are you supposed to do when you're waiting around in a hallway? But nothing on it interests me—I still don't have any friends besides Shireen and Mr. Monaghan, and they're both right here. I should text my mom—it's almost nine o'clock, and even though I know she's working late tonight, she's probably going to be home soon, and I don't want her to worry.

Except I'm not sure what to tell her. I don't know what she'll think about the fact that I'm here. There's probably an equal chance that she's an orangeshirt *or* a blueshirt—she and Debbie Monaghan are friends, but she also really admires Father Mosier. If I tell her that I'm at the Capitol, she'll probably know what's going on here—and man, would that be a stressful conversation. I don't even know how I'd answer her questions about which side I'm on.

Ran into some people I know, I type, deciding my best bet is to keep it vague. *I'll be back late.* A conversation tomorrow about how I spent the day bouncing between hanging out with Shireen and hanging out with Cassie sounds less awkward than a conversation with my Catholic mom about abortion.

Even though I am legally required to do community service, my mom mostly trusts me. She knows I'm not going to hang out with Jacob and Tommy again, and I'm sure she can tell I've been lonely. So when she responds, it's just to say: *cool. pizza in fridge if ur hungry.* Like I'm going to want more pizza anytime soon.

When Shireen returns from the bathroom, the black streaks are gone, and she's got her usual heavy eye makeup back on. I guess if you're a girl like Shireen, you know how to do that stuff fast.

"Let's go up to the auditorium," she says. "I could use a change of scenery."

We wind our way up the stairs. The auditorium is packed still, but there are a pair of open seats near the back. On the screen, one of the Republican state senators gets up—the guy who was talking to Wendy Davis earlier, when I was upstairs with Cassie—and David Dewhurst asks him why he's standing.

"To ask Senator Davis some questions," the senator says. "Would she yield?"

"I'm not yielding for any questions at this point, thank you," Wendy Davis says. But before she can continue, another senator—a woman I don't think has spoken today—also stands up.

"Senator Deuell, Senator does not yield," Dewhurst says. "Senator Nelson, for what purpose?"

"Well, I was going to ask if the gentlelady would yield," the woman says.

"I don't wish to yield for a question at this time," Wendy Davis responds.

Nelson doesn't seem to take that as an answer, though—she remains standing and turns to Dewhurst. "Mr. President, may I ask the gentlelady if there is any point this evening that she will yield for some questions from another woman?"

"I may do that, but I am not yielding for a question at this time," Wendy Davis says.

Shireen turns to me. "That's such bullshit. Playing the 'she's silencing women' card right now—like Wendy Davis is the one who's been anti-woman."

I hadn't even noticed that's what Senator Nelson was doing, but Wendy Davis sure is getting interrupted a lot.

I listen to her talk for a bit, if only just to get a break. You're having a particularly weird and hard day when you want to listen to a state senator talk at length about abortion and "irreversible physical impairments of a major bodily function" as, like, a way to just take your mind off things, but that is exactly the kind of day that I've been having.

Shireen seems just about as exhausted as I am. The rest of the room is mostly orange, except for a cluster of blues near the front. They must care a lot to spend all day in a space where they're outnumbered and people can just look at them and tell that they're the enemy. I wonder if there are parts of the Capitol full of blueshirts, and if the blues up front all knew each other before they got here, or if they banded together because they're so vastly outnumbered.

Whichever it is, they seem annoyed once Wendy Davis starts talking about another state senator, whose name is enough to get the orangeshirts to cheer. A hiss comes from the blues at the outburst.

"I see that Senator Van de Putte has joined the body this evening. We're so happy to have Senator Van de Putte on the floor, and we of course all share in the pain she's going through right now," Wendy Davis says.

Every time she says "Senator Van de Putte," the orangeshirts cheer. Most of them must be cheering just because other people are cheering, right? There can't be a ton of people who are, like, such big fans of a state senator that they'll cheer for her like she's Beyoncé. But even Shireen shouts a big "Woooooo!" like she just watched Senator Van de Putte sink a three-pointer at the buzzer.

Wendy Davis goes on to talk about how Senator Van de Putte is a pharmacist and has ideas about abortion-inducing drugs, and I lean over to Shireen. "What's the deal with her?"

"Oh, man," she says. "Her dad died in a car accident, and she missed a big vote because she was at the funeral. Those assholes used her dead dad to try to get their bill passed. She was with her family all day today—I guess she came late."

Oh, so it's that lady. It makes me think of Cassie, and I wonder how she's doing. Shireen and I have had our own unique hell to deal with, but at least we've had pizza and bathroom breaks.

"She didn't even have to be here today," Shireen says, and for half a second, I think she means Cassie, but of course she means Senator Van de Putte. "There aren't any more votes happening, just the filibuster, but here she is."

Wendy Davis continues talking about abortion pills, when a woman dressed in black, with a short, severe haircut and dark glasses, stands up on the floor.

"If you'll excuse me for a moment—Senator Campbell, for what purpose do you rise?" David Dewhurst asks the woman.

"Will the gentlewoman yield for questions?"

"I'll not yield at this time, thank you, Mr. President," Wendy Davis says.

"Senator Davis declines to yield," he tells the woman, because apparently politics means that you have to say things to people who are standing right there and can hear for themselves just fine.

"Um, even to a female and a physician?" the

woman—Campbell— says. I glance at Shireen, who's got her fighting face on as the "even to a female" line gets said again.

Wendy Davis looks at Dewhurst like, "Uhh, what'd I just say?" and he steps in. "The Senator has declined to yield."

"Thank you, Mr. President," Senator Campbell says, but she looks furious as she bites out a "thank you for your consideration" to Wendy Davis.

I pull my phone out and glance at the time—9:10, just under three hours to go. Shireen is looking at Twitter, I guess to get a feel for what to make of that weird exchange. Whatever is on her phone, she's engrossed in it. She pulls her thumb down, I guess to refresh her app, then shakes her head in rage and frustration.

"We have to get up there," she says, turning to me. "Donna Campbell is going to kill the filibuster. She's going to do it right now."

9:11 pm

"What?" I say. "How can she do that? How do you know?" My blood turns unexpectedly cold, and I feel a surge of adrenaline.

Shireen taps her phone. "There are, like, legislative aides. I'm following people who know them on Twitter. Apparently, Campbell has just decided to call whatever point of order she wants, and they're all going to vote for it. They're just going to wait for a few minutes to get a pretense."

I find myself immediately jumping to my feet. "Let's go," I say, and we step over the knees of the people sitting next to us to get to the aisle, then we take off up the stairs and out to the rotunda.

As we get to the gallery line, though, it's clear that we are never going to be able to get in. It's full of people in orange, all desperately waiting for a chance. A few hours ago, there were maybe fifty or sixty people waiting. Now there are hundreds and hundreds, all hoping that everybody who is currently in the gallery is going to get up or get raptured or something before the filibuster gets killed.

It's a helpless, desperate feeling—weirdly like the feeling you get when you're driving Jacob Kohler's Mustang and you realize that the directions he's giving you are to your former best friend's house, or the feeling you get when your best friend dies a few months after you stop talking to him so you never get a chance to make it right. It's the feeling you get when you've figured out what it is you actually care about, and it's too late to do anything about it.

I imagine if Shireen hadn't been able to get an abortion, if she couldn't be here because she was getting ready to have a baby that she didn't have a choice in carrying, because a bunch of senators she's never even met made a law that decided for her. Would she even be going to school in the fall? That David Dewhurst and Donna Campbell and whoever else would get to take the right to decide away from her just seems absurd to me. I don't know whether life begins at conception, or even if abortion is right or wrong, but it seems suddenly like we're so busy thinking about these big-picture questions that we forget we're talking about real people like Shireen and their actual lives.

Suddenly, the answers to all the questions I've been asking—and the big ones, not just the ones that came up in the past twelve hours——seem clear to me. *What's important to me?* and *What kind of person do I want to be?* and, maybe most importantly, *Do I have the courage to stand up for what I think is right?*

Because I know Jacob Kohler was wrong when he said I was a piece of shit. I know Mr. Monaghan was right when he said I need to be the good person that I know I can be, and not the asshole that I have in me sometimes. And Cassie, up there in her blue dress, saying she didn't think I believed in anything——that can't be the person I am. Hanging around, wearing my dirty white T-shirt, and leaving Shireen to deal with all of this alone? That's not the person I want to be.

"We've got to get in there," I say to Shireen, and she nods like, "Duh," but also like, "Yeah, but there are a million people here ahead of us in line."

"I don't think it's going to happen," she sighs.

"Come on," I say. "I know someone who might be able to help."

I know what side I'm on, so I pull off my shirt—which leaves Shireen staring at me like "what the hell"——and reach into my bag to pull out the orange T-shirt that reads "Stand with Texas Women." I ball up my white tee, throw it in the trash, and pull the orange shirt down over my head.

* * *

We're bolting up the stairs now, taking them two at a time, which is weird, because the entire day has been defined by the fact that it's supposed to go on forever, with no need to hurry. But here we are, a couple of teenagers bounding up the crowded staircases and hoping we can get inside the Senate gallery to bear witness as this cause that we both believe in has its last stand. We may not be able to make a difference, but we can watch. That means something.

We get to the third floor, and the line is full of anxious people. Some of them are looking at their phones, while others are staring desperately at the door, like they might be able to will eight hundred extra seats into existence.

And there, up at the front of the line——the very next people to get in——are Mr. Monaghan and his lady friend Constance, leaning against the wall and looking tired.

"You're still here!" I say to Mr. Monaghan.

"There's our man!" he says, like he does in the morning before I read to him from *A Game of Thrones*. "We've been up here this long, why move now?"

"I need to ask you a favor," I say. "It's a big one." I take a deep breath, because this is going to be hard to say out loud in front of Shireen. But the sort of person I want to be will say things that are hard to talk about if they're important. "I was thinking about what you said earlier, and I——"

Mr. Monaghan holds up a hand like he knows what I'm about to ask, so I stop, because I didn't know how to ask it anyway. He looks at us, then at Constance.

She nods. "It sounds like the seats in there are murder on your back anyway."

Shireen looks at Constance like she's bathed in yellow light. "Are you sure? You must have been up here for hours."

"What the hell, honey?" Constance laughs. "I've fought this battle before. It's your turn now."

Shireen throws her arms around Constance, who hugs her back. I think Mr. Monaghan gives me a nod of approval, but he might just be getting sleepy.

Shireen turns to the woman from Oklahoma who I talked to earlier—the woman standing behind Mr. Monaghan and Constance in line—and says, "Is it totally unfair if we swap spots with them?"

The woman from Oklahoma thinks for a second, then shrugs. "I guess not. There were two people ahead of me in line before, and there are two people ahead of me in line now."

Shireen hugs her, too. "We're not going to let them get away with this," she says.

The woman from Oklahoma nods. "I don't know

how we'll stop them, but they'll for damn sure know we're watching."

As if on cue, an old woman—small and hunched, wearing an orange shirt—walks out the doors, with someone who must be her granddaughter helping her. The DPS trooper at the door turns to us and says, "Next two," and Mr. Monaghan looks at me and Shireen.

"Go if you're going," he says, and I nod. I stick out my hand to shake, and Mr. Monaghan takes it. It feels like a significant gesture. There are two kinds of people in this world, I figure—those who Mr. Monaghan respects enough to shake their hand, and those he really, really, *really* does not, and I feel like I belong in the first camp right now.

Then Shireen and I enter the Senate gallery, which is suddenly the most intense room I have ever been in in my entire life.

9:40 pm

The entire Senate Chamber is basically silent when we walk in. There's some quiet chatter from people in the gallery, but down on the floor, everything is quiet. Wendy Davis is still there, still standing, but she's not talking. Over at David Dewhurst's podium, there's a small army of people—including Donna Campbell—all talking about the rules.

We grab the pair of vacant seats and sit on the edges of the cushions, craning to be a few inches closer to the floor where whatever it is they're discussing is being discussed, even though we are on a different level of the building and like a hundred feet away.

Two guys, probably in their twenties, sit in front of us—they look like a couple—and Shireen taps one on the shoulder.

"What's going on?" she asks the one with spiky blond hair.

"The evil sorceress down there called the third point of order. The last POO." His eyes flash with recognition as he looks at Shireen. "Oh, *hey*! I saw you earlier. You have the amazing shirt. I'm Ian," he says, sticking out his hand. "This is Brantley." He gestures to his companion, a really tall guy with a square jaw and red hair. We all do the handshake-and-names thing.

"So what was the POO about?" Shireen asks.

"Nothing. Literally nothing," Ian says. "Wendy was talking about how the bill would make it take three doctor's appointments to do something that should take one, because of the BS sonogram bill they passed last time. And then Donna Campbell down there said that saying the word *sonogram* isn't germane. Wendy explained that, like, she was talking about how the current law just makes this new one even *harder*—she was *mad*, you can tell—and then Dewhurst called everybody over to talk about it."

"The fix is in," Brantley says, shaking his head with disgust. "We were so close—it's, what, almost ten o'clock? She had this in the bag."

"Shireen saw on Twitter—they decided to kill the filibuster, they were just waiting for the time to do it," I say.

It feels good sitting here with Shireen, Ian, and Brantley, not to mention the orange army assembled throughout the gallery. There's nothing wrong with belonging—you just have to belong with the right people.

My phone buzzes in my pocket. I pull it out—it's a text from Cassie.

I see you made it back in.

I look around the room and find the small pocket of blue all the way across the gallery. I can see Marsha and, of course, Cassie in her blue dress. She's looking right at me with a hurt expression. I glance down at my orange shirt.

I'm sorry, I text back. Not for wearing the orange shirt, and not for taking off the blue one. I'm just sorry her feelings are hurt. *Can we talk later?*

I don't know what there is to talk about.

I avoided Jacob Kohler and Tommy Richman for months, and I nearly skipped an elevator ride this morning because I saw Shireen in it. I was afraid to talk to them all because I was ashamed of what I'd done. Now I *want* to talk to Cassie because I'm not ashamed. But I guess it's like Mr. Monaghan said—if she doesn't want to hear it, then I have to let it go.

Shireen glances my way. "Trouble in paradise?"

"It's not like that," I say. For the first time, I realize that I don't even *want* it to be like that. So what if I'm not the person Cassie thought I was? Sitting here in the Senate gallery with Shireen, it's clear the person Cassie thought I was isn't the person I want to be. He seems like a good guy, that Alex Collins—but I can be a different sort of good guy, too.

Shireen seems to accept my answer, because she gives me a frustrated, tight-lipped smile and moves on to "What the hell is going on down there?"

"A miscarriage of democracy," a woman sitting in the row behind us says. She's probably my mom's age, and she sits with a man in an orange T-shirt. "I'm Jolene."

We trade names with her and her husband, Josh, who's a lawyer. They've got kids, too—two of them, both little girls, playing games on an iPad.

"What can we do?" I ask, even though I know that there's nothing we *can* do. "This isn't right."

"It's not right," Jolene says. "But it's Texas. What we can do is elect better people."

"That doesn't do us any good right now," I say.

"It's not up to us," Josh says. "It's up to them. It always is, in the end." He gestures to the Senate floor, where there's still an ongoing conference at David Dewhurst's desk while Wendy Davis keeps on standing, waiting with the rest of us to see if they can really get away with this.

* * *

It turns out, they really *can* get away with this. After something like half an hour of waiting and watching and chatting and looking at Twitter—Lena Dunham tweeted #StandWithWendy, and Shireen gushed, because she loves *Girls* as much as I love *Game of Thrones*—everybody finally returns to their places, and Dewhurst bangs his gavel.

"Members, after consultation with the parliamentarian and after going over what people heard, as far as discussion—Senator Campbell, your point of order is well taken, and is sustained."

He bangs his gavel again, but you can't hear it from where I'm sitting because the entire gallery erupts in boos. It's *loud*. I look around—are the police coming? But they're not. Another senator stands, and he starts talking even as the entire room continues booing and shouting. Even with his microphone, I can barely make out his words.

"I move to concur with the House amendment to Senate Bill 5," the senator says.

On the other side of the chamber, Kirk Watson—my state senator, the meme guy—stands up. In front of me, Brantley shouts "Bullshit!" really loudly. I expect to see cops, but there's still nothing.

Dewhurst slams his gavel down three times, but everybody starts chanting, "Let her speak! Let her speak!"

Shireen shouts "Let her speak!" too, and pumps her first in the sky the same way she did when we saw the Black Keys and they played "Lonely Boy." Ian and Brantley do the same, and I find my own voice, too—"Let her speak! Let her speak!"—and it goes on and on, all of us chanting "Let her speak!" for a full minute, because it feels good to let them know—all of them down there at their desks—that we're here, that we're watching, that we know what it is they're trying to get away with.

The chanting finally dies out when Dewhurst addresses Kirk Watson and Watson begins to talk. Starting practically every sentence with the words *parliamentary inquiry*, Watson explains that David Dewhurst had said earlier that after the third strike, the decision would come down to the Senate over whether to end the filibuster—that Dewhurst couldn't make that decision himself. I don't really get what the difference would be, but I've spent the day learning that parliamentary procedure is super important to all of the people down there, so there must be one. As if to affirm that, somebody on the other side of the gallery shouts, "Yeah!"

Dewhurst talks to the parliamentarian again, and this all feels very precarious. But then Ian and Brantley start chanting, "Wendy! Wendy!" and Shireen and I get in on it, and suddenly the entire room takes it up. We're breaking the law, I guess, because we were already warned that we could go to jail for making a disruption—but it feels too good to stop.

Kirk Watson keeps explaining to David Dewhurst how the Texas Senate rules work. "Once you've made a determination that there are three warnings, or whatever you want to call it—that matter must then be submitted to the body to determine if there will be an end to the filibuster."

I look over at Shireen, who's glued to Twitter.

"He's right," she says. "At least, that's what all the people on Twitter are saying. Dewhurst can call the third strike, but then the Senate has to decide what to do with it."

Dewhurst talks to the parliamentarian again. I'm waiting for something to happen—something to chant, something to watch—when Kirk Watson speaks. "I move that the ruling of the chair be over-ruled, and I seek to appeal the ruling of the chair."

Everybody in orange immediately loses it. It feels like we're at a football game, and our team just recovered a fumble. Suddenly, there's a glimmer of hope.

Kirk Watson looks up to the gallery, then delivers his next line with flourish. "It's my understanding that this is a debatable motion?"

Dewhurst sags like he's just completely exhausted and says, "That is correct."

We all start clapping and cheering—including me, even though I barely understand what's happening.

"What does that mean?" I ask Shireen or Ian or Brantley or Jolene or Josh or the little kids playing *Angry Birds* or anybody else.

"It means he can do his own little filibuster-within-the-filibuster," Josh says, and Shireen grabs my arm real tight, because this isn't finished yet.

10:20 pm

This is what my day has come to: At nine o'clock this morning, the most excitement I expected to encounter today was reading to Mr. Monaghan about what sort of shenanigans were going on in King's Landing. After that, I figured that I would go home to spend many quality hours with my Xbox. Instead, I've attended the first political protest of my life for a cause that, until maybe an hour ago, I didn't even have an opinion on. I've established a surprisingly deep emotional connection with Cassie Ramirez, who is the sort of girl that the phrase "out of my league" was coined for. I've decided that—beautiful and smart and funny and fascinating though she may be—I'm actually not that into her, which is great, because she pretty much hates me now. Meanwhile, I've made amends with my enemy, Shireen Dehghan, and now we're in the gallery overlooking the Texas Senate Chamber, watching as Kirk Watson attempts to begin a two-hour-and-forty-minute filibuster, riveted by the entire proceedings before us like we are watching the season finale of *Game of Thrones* or maybe the goddamn Super Bowl.

So it's been a day.

On the Senate floor, Kirk Watson prepares to ramble about Senate rules or something. Honestly, I have no idea how any of this works. I *would* feel super uneducated, except I've learned in the past eleven hours that actual members of the Texas Senate don't know any more than I do, so what the heck? Even David Dewhurst, the guy who is supposed to be in charge of everything, keeps staring at his iPad and poring over the rules like he just became president of the Senate five minutes ago after he won a sweepstakes on the back of a package of M&Ms.

Eventually, Dewhurst bangs his gavel twice and announces that, because Kirk Watson is appealing a motion *he* introduced, he's going to step down as chair and put some senator named Duncan in charge in his place.

They hold a quick conversation at Dewhurst's desk, and then Duncan addresses me and Shireen and the rest of the people in the gallery. "All right, members and persons in the gallery, if you could listen to me very closely. Lieutenant Governor Dewhurst, at the beginning of the session today, read the rules with regard to the decorum required in the Senate. This is a very serious issue. This is a very serious debate. You are here to observe, and the members cannot accurately debate with disruptions in the chamber. So there will be strict enforcement with regard to disruptions in the chamber, so that the Senate can debate this important issue."

Another senator, who I recognize as Leticia Van de Putte—at this point, I can recognize many of my state senators on sight, just like every other teenager can—stands to speak, but Duncan keeps on rolling.

"If there is another outburst as we observed earlier," he says, "then we will request that the gallery be cleared."

Leticia Van de Putte, whose day has been bad enough since it was also her father's funeral, keeps saying, "Mr. President? Mr. President?" until Duncan finally recognizes her.

"What purpose?" he asks, and she says the two words I've gotten very used to hearing from my state senators today: "Parliamentary inquiry."

The gallery is quiet now, because we don't want to get kicked out—as boring as most "parliamentary inquiries" tend to be, we're absolutely riveted, because this isn't actually about parliamentary inquiries or whatever they're actually going to talk about, just like Wendy Davis's filibuster wasn't actually about having a very long, mostly one-sided debate about abortion that was just going to coincidentally last until 12:01 in the morning. Instead, it's a very weird competition in which one side makes up all of the rules as they go, and the other side has to try to beat them by making totally unexpected plays in the spaces created by the shifting rules.

And that's exactly what Leticia Van de Putte does as she talks to the new temporary president of the Texas Senate—she asks him to fill her in on the processes that played out before she got here, since she came in late.

Senator Duncan doesn't seem all that interested in her request. He tells her that "the process is the process for a filibuster stated in the rules," and she follows up, starting every question with the words *parliamentary inquiry*, which she enunciates slowly. Because there's nothing else to do, I take out my phone and run the stopwatch timer as I whisper the words *parliamentary inquiry* in roughly the same cadence. It takes 2.39 seconds, which means that if she makes twenty-five parliamentary inquiries, then just saying those words will eat up another minute of the hundred that are left before the special legislative session is over and the abortion bill—which would make it all but impossible for Shireen and all the other girls, women, transgender guys, and nonbinary people who need an abortion to get one——ends up defeated.

So, that's what's going on in the Senate Chamber, as we wait for Kirk Watson and Leticia Van de Putte to play Luigi to Wendy Davis's Mario and carry this filibuster through the finish line. They have 100 minutes to fill, and it doesn't matter even a little bit how they fill them, just as long as they do.

Van de Putte mentions that she was at her father's funeral and that she'd like to know what the three points of order that ended Wendy Davis's filibuster were. "I was not here, and I do not know," she says. "And I was not looking online, because I was at my father's funeral."

The reminder that her dad just died is enough to get Duncan to sigh and recap what went down earlier in the day: that a Senator Nichols who looks like a creepy Santa Claus called a point of order that was strike one because Wendy Davis brought up the state's budget; and that a Senator Williams who I never got a look at called a second point of order that was strike two because one of the other Democrats helped Davis put on a friggin' back brace. Leticia Van de Putte was here for the third point of order, so she doesn't get to eat up any time with that one.

Van de Putte doesn't appear to be finished, but

another senator—a big guy—stands up, and they both say "Mr. President" at the same time.

Duncan looks at the guy and says, "Senator Estes, for what purpose?"

Estes starts saying, "I motion to . . ." when another guy, this one named Whitmire, stands up and says, "Parliamentary inquiry."

"That's so smart," I whisper to Shireen. "Every time one of them says 'parliamentary inquiry,' it eats up, like, three seconds from the clock."

Shireen, who's been staring at Twitter for the past few minutes, shakes her head. "That's not why they're doing it." She gestures to her phone's screen like it's the source of all knowledge, which I guess it basically is. "It's because the rules say that a parliamentary inquiry gives them the right to talk first, before anybody else goes."

"So this guy—he's on our side, right?" I ask.

"This guy is," she says, pointing to Whitmire. "This guy isn't." She points to Senator Estes.

Whitmire goes on to talk some more parliamentary nonsense about the rules. While I have no idea what any of it means, I don't need to know. My phone says he's eaten another minute from the clock.

They go on and on—Whitmire asking questions that he already knows the answers to, Duncan answering them with the things that Whitmire already knows—and it takes up another minute. Meanwhile, I can hear a chant start: "Let us in! Let us in!" It makes me nervous—Duncan isn't going to have the police kick us out, is he?—before I realize that they're saying "let us in" because they're actually *outside* the heavy doors that make up the entrance to the Senate Chamber.

As the chant dies out, so does Whitmire's inquiry. Duncan says, "Senator Estes has the floor," and I realize that we're about to get screwed again.

"What about Kirk Watson?" I ask Shireen. She shakes her head, like she doesn't know, either.

I'm not the only one who's wondering—I see it on the faces of our new friends Jolene and Josh behind us, and Ian and Brantley in front of us, and all throughout the gallery. I see it on Shireen's phone, too, in the angry tweets saying things like "Watson never yielded the floor," which is a collection of words that would not have made sense to me on any other day, but which today makes sense not only to me, but to a hundred thousand other people all over the world who are watching this.

"Who's that guy?" I ask of the person who tweeted about Watson, and Shireen shrugs, then taps her finger on his picture. It's someone with a yellow avatar, whose location is listed as Vancouver, British

Columbia. Every random weirdo on Twitter is following what's happening here right now.

On the Senate floor, they're now debating whose turn it is, and whether Watson yielded the floor or if he was just interrupted by Leticia Van de Putte because she had parliamentary inquiries and those go first.

It's partly fascinating to watch, because the results matter a lot—if they decide that Watson yielded the floor, then dozens of abortion clinics will close and people like Shireen will be out of luck. It's also partly really boring, because it's a bunch of politicians bickering over the rules to some really complicated game. For most of the day, "fascinating and boring" has been my general reaction to all of this. It's been like watching poker on TV, where the stakes are high and the tension is mounting, but everybody keeps getting dealt crappy hands so all the stuff that actually makes poker interesting to watch never happens.

But now, I'm not bored *or* fascinated. Now, watching as this day comes down to weird games and debates over "did Watson yield the floor" make me *furious*—they're acting like theoretical questions about procedure are more important than the actual impact that this bill is going to have on real people's lives.

Another senator—Rodney Ellis, whose name I

remember because he was the guy who helped put Wendy Davis's back brace on earlier—gets in on the action, demanding that Duncan check the transcripts of the debate, or that they watch the video, so they can check to make sure that Kirk Watson didn't yield the floor right after he said "this is a debatable motion," even though I know—and the other 499 people in this gallery know, and the one hundred thousand people watching online know—that he didn't, since we were all paying very close attention.

The entire room looks ready to riot. All I can see are people sitting on the edges of their uncomfortable seats, ready to pounce and, I dunno, jump however many feet down to deliver flying elbow drops onto Duncan or Estes or whoever's fault it would be if they shove this bill through by breaking the rules. I look over at the section of blueshirts and try to catch Cassie's eye—but she and Marsha and the other blues don't seem to be interested in making eye contact with anybody in orange.

Then Duncan says that Senator Estes has been recognized on a motion to table debate, even though it's not his turn yet, and I feel like all the air has been sucked out of my lungs, like the past eleven hours have been wasted and I've been watching a rigged game this whole time—when another state senator says the magic words *parliamentary inquiry,* and Duncan sighs.

"Senator West, state your inquiry," he says.

"Is *your* decision appealable?" he asks.

11:05 pm

We've gone from spending the day watching Wendy Davis—who Shireen and most of the other orangeshirts call "Wendy," like they're best friends, and who Cassie calls "that woman"—talk on and on in an attempt to kill the bill by boring it to death, to watching a ragtag group of state senators none of us have ever heard of as they try to keep the ball in the air.

Wendy Davis is still on the Senate floor, still standing, while all of this goes down. I can't help it—I look over at Cassie again, who I know hasn't had anything to eat or drink in the past twelve hours. It makes me wish that we were on the same side, because I really do want to be friends with her. I haven't had any friends who aren't foul-mouthed octogenarians for a while now, and I want to build for myself a group that involves the best people I know—and that's Shireen, and it's also Cassie. I wouldn't be here without her.

On the floor, West and Duncan go back and forth

about what the rules are, and what's debatable, and it's like watching Calvin and Hobbes argue about which tree you have to run three circles around to score in Calvinball.

I turn to Shireen. "This must be riveting broadcasting for the people watching on the internet."

"Says here that a hundred forty thousand people are watching," she says.

"Holy crap. Are you learning anything else important from Twitter?"

She shakes her head. "There isn't really anything else to learn. I'm just staring at it because I'm going to lose it, dude. This is so friggin' ridiculous."

She locks her phone screen and palms it, then stares down at the Senate floor, where a female senator who has white hair and looks a little like an older version of Debbie Monaghan is talking. After a few seconds, Shireen unlocks her phone, refreshes Twitter, reads the five new tweets that came up since she locked it, and palms it again.

I feel basically the same anxiety that Shireen seems to right now, but I don't have the same stake in this that she does. It's hard to watch her stressing about this and feeling helpless. "Helpless" was never something that came to mind when I thought about Shireen. Part of the reason I wasn't always super excited about her and Jesse being together is that she intimidated me.

I'm not intimidated now. I *do* think that it's possible that she could leap over the safety railing, land on all fours on the Senate floor, look up menacingly, pounce on Senator Estes, and rip his throat out with her teeth, but that doesn't intimidate me so much as it reminds me of how badass she is. I realize that today might be the first time I've seen Shireen for herself, rather than just as Jesse's girlfriend. Part of that hurts—Jesse's gone, so of course I don't see her as Jesse's girlfriend—but part of it makes me feel like I'm doing the things Mr. Monaghan told me I should. Shireen was never just "Jesse's girlfriend" when he was alive and they were together. But I was too angry to let her be anything more than that.

Shireen stuffs her phone into her back pocket and exhales slowly and loudly, like she's doing yoga or trying to breathe her way through this. On the floor, the state senator who reminds me of Debbie Monaghan bleeds more and more time off the clock by arguing that the Senate rules require all three strikes to be about what's germane, not two strikes on what's germane and one strike about whether back braces are allowed. She's going to lose—I've seen enough go down today to know that no "debate" will actually change anybody's mind or vote on anything—but it's not about winning, it's just about milking that clock. The longer she talks, the better—and what she says doesn't matter to anybody except for the scorekeepers.

After a few minutes, Duncan axes her questions, too. I look over to Shireen, who's on the verge of tears, and it hits me just how much we've been through together and how, if I hadn't been here today, she might be watching this on her own—or at least without anyone who knows how personal this is for her, and how hard it is to be stuck while what's important to you careens out of control.

Senator Duncan tells Kirk Watson that it's his time to make closing remarks, because apparently whoever is right or wrong doesn't matter at this point—they have forty-five minutes to pass this bill, and if that means cutting him off even though it's against their own weird rules, they'll go ahead and cut him off, and nothing anybody says will change their mind.

Kirk Watson begins his monologue, but I have a hard time focusing on it, because I'm thinking about a night months and months ago, in the fall, at the garage apartment behind Jesse's house.

Jesse and Shireen had gotten into a big, blowup fight before school that morning. I had worked a late shift at Double Dave's the night before—I was picking up extra shifts, just to have a place to put my-self—so I only saw the aftermath. Our whole friend group was a little shell-shocked. When I saw Jesse in second period English class, I asked him about it.

"I don't know," he said. "This sucks. I just want things to go back to how they used to be."

It was a huge relief to hear him say that. We still hung out sometimes after school, when things were calmer, but I hadn't come by the garage apartment on the weekend since that awful night at the start of the school year when all those older dudes were there with the pills. I loved the idea of things going back to how they used to be.

"I could come by after work, maybe?" I said. "Bring a pizza, and me, you, and Bobby could watch a movie?"

"Yeah," he said, his tone a little faraway. "That would be nice."

When I got to work, I asked Arno if I could be one of the early cuts, and since I hadn't asked for that in a long time, he said sure. I made my once-per-shift take-home pizza, strapped it to my bike rack with a bungee cord, and was on my bike heading toward Jesse's a little after ten o'clock.

I soon realized this was a silly idea. There were at least a half-dozen cars parked on the street in front of the house as I rode up.

I went inside. Maybe twelve people were hanging out. I thought I had seen five of them before. Some guy I didn't know said, "Whoa, did we order a pizza?" And when I kept coming in, he added, "Is the pizza guy gonna party with us?"

"Nah, that's Alex," Jesse said. "He doesn't party with us."

The way he said it, it was like I had hurt *his* feelings. But maybe that was just Jesse now.

I put the pizza on the coffee table, and Jesse turned to Bobby. "Dude, when is your cousin getting here? Is he really going to have coke?"

"Soon, my brother," Bobby said, a spaced-out grin on his face. "Soon."

I was officially in over my head. I imagined turning around and walking back out the door, because maybe I *was* just the pizza guy. But I kept walking toward the couch, resigning myself to a night of feeling sadder and lonelier than I would have felt if I hadn't gone at all.

More and more people came—it turned out that everyone wanted to get in on whatever Bobby's cousin was bringing over—and I sat there, the only person in the garage apartment watching *Let the Right One In* with the subtitles on and the sound off. Shireen and Holly came by after an hour or so. I guess she and Jesse *hadn't* broken up. A little while after that, some guy who looked like an older version of Bobby came in. Bobby went up to him, and they did a complicated handshake that also included Bobby slipping him a roll of cash.

Bobby's cousin took a bag of white powder into the kitchen. Jesse hovered around him like an eager student, hoping to watch as he cut it into lines or something, whatever it is people do with cocaine in movies. I didn't want to watch, so I went outside on the balcony, where nobody else was because it was October in Texas and almost a hundred degrees even in the middle of the night and anyway, all of the coke was inside.

I stared out at the street that ran in front of the main house and imagined getting on my bike and riding home, waking up my mom, and telling her everything. But I knew I wouldn't do it. So I just stood there and felt sorry for myself.

After a minute, the door opened.

"Hey," Shireen said. "It's friggin' *hot* out here."

"It's cooler inside," I said, nodding my head right back toward the door she had just come through. I didn't know why she was there; I'd figured she would be inside lining up with Jesse and Bobby.

Shireen shook her head. "It's crowded, though."

"Somebody should tell them to go home, then," I said, looking at her pointedly.

She looked like maybe I'd hurt her feelings, which didn't make sense to me. Weren't they *her* people? Then she put her elbows on the wrought-iron railing next to me and looked out onto the street that, a few months later, I would drive Jacob Kohler's car down before he'd throw a brick through her window.

"Maybe they'll go home tomorrow," she said. "Maybe we can do something more low-key after that."

There was no way that would happen, I knew that now. That wasn't what anybody except for me, and apparently Shireen, wanted, and nobody cared about "low-key" anymore. So we just stood on the balcony, sweat beading on our foreheads in the middle of the night, enjoying the breeze when it came, nobody inside missing either one of us.

11:34 pm

Sitting in the Senate gallery, I remember feeling that night that Shireen and I knew something that nobody else did. I even remember feeling a little less alone.

But I also remember burying those feelings because I was too hurt and too angry with everybody to let myself feel them. I remember deciding later that the only way to stop feeling sorry for myself was to start hanging out with Jacob and Tommy, trash-talk my friends behind their backs, and go along with whatever awful shit Jacob and Tommy wanted to do to them. That I could only let my hurt go once I felt like I had done something bad to them, too.

Now I realize that Shireen and I could have been friends this whole time, real friends, and maybe if we had, it could have made a difference. It's too late for that to matter for Jesse, but maybe it can make a difference here.

On the floor, Kirk Watson has been talking for at least ten minutes. He's pulled out a big book of

Senate rules, and he's reading excerpts from it— long excerpts, as he attempts to draw this thing out. And I want him to, desperately, but I'm also getting frustrated, because he's talking about rules and not about the people who this is for. He's not talking about how Shireen's whole life would be different if she hadn't been able to get an abortion. He's not talking about how she'd probably be a single mom right now, raising the unwanted baby of her dead ex-boyfriend. He's not talking about how her body and her life would be transformed forever because of one night when her birth control didn't do its job, or how maybe she wouldn't even be in school anymore, wouldn't be starting to apply to colleges, wouldn't be doing all the things that should be part of her life, because she wouldn't have had a choice in the matter.

All of that stuff matters, but it's not what Kirk Watson is talking about. He's got his big book out and he's talking about tabling a motion to appeal, whatever that means, and how that'll end the filibuster.

"I don't believe it's appropriate to end the filibuster without a vote of the body," he says. "I think that's what we've been promised and told in rulings all day today, and I think that rule requires that there be three findings of not-germaneness, as opposed to what we've had here today." He goes on and on—he really stretches this out, and I'm grateful for every second he spends talking—but I realize, now, that it's not going to be enough.

Shireen, who's been slumped in her chair, moves to sit up. My phone says it's 11:36, which means there are twenty-four minutes to go, and we're not going to make it, because the game is rigged and most of the people on that floor are men who don't have to ever think about the things that Shireen had to think about when she found out that she was pregnant. I try not to look too disappointed, because I don't want to spread my negativity to Shireen, but of course she's already thinking the same thing.

"He's not going to make it," she whispers to me. She's got tears in her eyes, big ones welling up, as Senator Estes stands up.

"For what purpose, Senator Estes?" Duncan says.

"I would like to move the previous question."

This is the moment we've been dreading—the moment of defeat. Duncan asks another parliamentary question about "do you have five Seconds," Estes names five other senators, and Duncan begins to take the vote.

"What's happening?" I ask Shireen, my voice a panic.

From behind me, Josh explains in a hushed tone, "They're about to vote on ending the debate on Watson's appeal. That would let them vote on whether to end the filibuster, and then to vote on whether to pass the bill."

"How long will all of that take?" Shireen's voice is even more tense than mine.

Josh shakes his head. "Just a couple of minutes," he says, sounding resigned.

Before they start casting the votes, though, Kirk Watson speaks up again: "Parliamentary inquiry, Mr. President."

He goes back to his original point—that it was his turn, when he was speaking earlier, and he hadn't yielded—but nobody gives a shit about that, just like every other rule here. Duncan instructs the secretary to start naming senators so they can vote, and then West, the Black guy who asked Duncan "is your decision appealable?" makes another parliamentary inquiry.

"Rule 6.03 requires that all motions shall be reduced to writing and read by the secretary if desired by the presiding officer, or any senator present," he says. "I desire that it be reduced to writing and read by the secretary."

Duncan sighs—I get the feeling that he would rather be anywhere else in the world right now than presiding over the Texas Senate—and says, "Senator Estes, you've heard the request of Senator West. Would you reduce your motion to writing?"

West adds, "It needs to be in as big a font as possible."

This is what we've come down to here—it's 11:38, and the Democrats are doing everything they can to stretch this out for the next twenty-two minutes, even making the Republicans write out their motions in big fonts. But if Josh is right, and their team needs only two minutes to pass the bill, then it's hard to imagine that our team has twenty minutes of stalling left in them. Watching what's happening down on the floor still feels a little bit like watching a football game, but now my team is down by two points, the refs are on the take, it's fourth down, and my guys have been called for six false start penalties in a row, so now we're doing an 80-yard field goal attempt. I look over to Shireen, who stares at her phone again like there's some hope to be found buried on Twitter.

"How are you doing?" I ask, even though I know how she's doing. I want her to know that I care.

"I feel so helpless," she says.

It sounds so strange to hear confident, unflappable Shireen say those words that I wonder if she's ever felt that way before—but then, I realize, of course she has. She watched what happened to Jesse, same as I did.

Kirk Watson makes another inquiry. While he takes his time spitting it out, I find myself thinking about Jesse again. Not about how abandoned I felt by him when things got druggy, not about Shireen and him—but *Jesse*, and how I never talked to him after the night with the brick and the window. I had so many bad feelings to swallow down, but he must have felt so betrayed, and when he and Bobby shot themselves up with whatever they shot themselves up with a few weeks later, he probably still felt like I hated him, or like he should hate me. The idea that my best friend died feeling like that is still something I can't handle.

I know that Shireen has her own feelings about all of this—about how she couldn't stop any of it, either—and all of our helplessness feels trapped in my throat as I watch Duncan shoot down Kirk Watson's inquiry and ignore Leticia Van de Putte, who's standing to be recognized and saying something I can't hear because her microphone is apparently not working.

"The secretary will call roll," Duncan says, and the secretary starts calling out names to vote.

"She's as screwed as we are," I say to Shireen.

"Nobody is listening to *any* of us," she whispers back.

Leticia Van de Putte keeps standing, and the secretary keeps reading names, and Duncan seems really annoyed now—he keeps saying "we're in the middle of a roll call" and "the secretary will continue to call roll" even as Van de Putte stands there trying to be recognized.

Finally, after the vote is tallied and, huge shock, Kirk Watson loses, Duncan lets Van de Putte talk.

"Parliamentary inquiry," she says, looking really depressed.

Seeing her get shut down seems to awaken something in everybody around me, though. We've all been sitting here in despair, but the seats start to buzz with energy again. It's like we've all realized that even if our team jumps through all the parliamentary hoops, the other team will just change the rules again. And that's what she and Duncan start arguing about—she accuses of him "throwing the rule book out on the floor," and he retorts, "Do you wish to make a motion?"

"I'm asking for a parliamentary inquiry, and a question of the chair—why was I not recognized?" she says.

Duncan says that she wasn't recognized because no one heard her, which seems like it can't possibly be true, since he kept interrupting her to tell her they were taking the vote. The whole thing is so impossibly frustrating that when someone across the gallery shouts "Bullshit!" I don't worry about going to jail. I just wish I had shouted it first.

Duncan gives Van de Putte the opportunity to

make whatever motion she wanted to make before the last vote, but she says that she doesn't want to make that motion now—she wanted to make it when she stood up to make it, and the rules say that she should have been able to.

Shireen looks like she might need to chew through her own arm to keep from screaming.

"These guys—these *men*—they won't even let her speak," she says. "They're going to take away our rights, and they're going to do it by acting like they don't even hear her." She looks like a bundle of nervous energy now, like she wants to cry and fight and scream all at once. But instead, she's stuck up here like I am—like we all are, even the ones on the Senate floor who are supposed to have the authority to do something about this.

"So now," Duncan says, "the issue before the body is the appeal of the presiding officer's ruling on the point of order related to germaneness as raised by Senator Campbell." In other words, now they're going to vote that *talking about abortion is off topic when talking about abortion.* "The secretary will call the roll."

It's the most painful ending I could have imagined. What a rip-off. I feel cheated, as does pretty much everybody else here. We all wasted our time today—or longer, since Shireen and Debbie Monaghan and probably a hundred others have been coming all week—to watch them play a game that was rigged from the beginning. The energy in the room is still there, but we're all just holding it with nowhere to direct it now.

The secretary calls roll, and the senators vote, and it goes exactly the way everyone knew it would. Duncan calls on another male senator to ask if there are five others who will second the motion, and he names five more senators. Leticia Van de Putte stands again, as does Kirk Watson, and Duncan calls on Watson. I look at my phone—it's 11:45. I can't imagine that even a guy who loves to hear himself talk as much as Kirk Watson seems to have fifteen more minutes of parliamentary inquiries in him. Meanwhile, Duncan isn't even talking to Leticia Van de Putte.

Watson asks another parliamentary inquiry— something about whether they should have to hold a vote to decide if the filibuster is officially over—and Duncan tells him that Dewhurst said that it was, and that's good enough for him. Van de Putte keeps standing, though, and finally Duncan acknowledges her.

"Senator Van de Putte, for what purpose?"

"Mr. President, parliamentary inquiry," she says as slowly as humanly possible. She then asks him a question that I barely understand about "if a member on the prevailing side of the motion can be recognized for a motion to reconsider the vote" and whether that means that motion takes precedence, which I think means that she's still upset that she was ignored when she tried to talk earlier and that he then said it was too late for her to be heard on what she'd wanted to say.

"We are on another motion at this time," Duncan says. "So it would not be in order at this time to reconsider the vote on a previous matter before the body"—which, after twelve hours of developing an ear for parliamentary speak, sounds a lot like "you snooze, you lose."

Except she *didn't* snooze. He ignored her, and there's no way she and Kirk Watson and the others on our side have another thirteen minutes of inquiries they can use to stretch this out past midnight.

Shireen is crying pretty hard now. When she sees me look over, she wraps her arms around me and buries her face in my chest. I hug her back, but I know there's nothing I can do, nothing either of us can do, and I'm so tired of that helpless feeling. I want to yell "bullshit!" like that guy did earlier, but so loudly that everyone stops and looks up at me and the cops come to take me away. I want to hurl Shireen directly at Duncan's head like a guided missile. I look around the room, and I see the same energy pulsing through everyone else. How can we all be this powerless?

On the floor, Leticia Van de Putte seems to feel the exact same way. I can hear her exhaustion when she says, "Mr. President, parliamentary inquiry."

"State your inquiry," Duncan says, with his own exhaustion dripping through his voice.

"At what point," Van de Putte asks, her voice suddenly strong and angry, "must a female senator raise her hand or her voice to be recognized over the male colleagues in the room?"

That's when we lose it.

Shireen jumps to her feet, and I'm right behind her—as are Ian and Brantley and Josh and Jolene and everybody else in the room who's wearing orange. We start cheering and clapping because someone finally *said* it—what we've all been feeling. It may not change anything, but it means so much to just *hear* it.

A funny thing happens as we cheer and clap and shout: when Duncan starts talking, he can't be heard. And when the secretary starts calling roll, even before she's halfway through naming the senators for the vote, her voice is completely drowned out and she gives up.

Duncan pounds his gavel, and I see him shout for "order, order," but I keep clapping, and I keep shouting. We all do, and it's the most important thing I've ever been a part of in my entire life. Soon I can't hear anything at all except for my own screaming, and Shireen's, and the hundreds of other people in the gallery, as we're all shouting and crying and yelling as loudly as we can.

My voice is raw after only thirty seconds, but I check the time on my phone—11:48, which means that I have to keep this up for another twelve minutes, because we all do. I look over to Shireen, who's got huge, joyful tears streaming down her face, and I put my phone away and touch my face and feel wetness and start screaming even louder.

I scream for Shireen, and for the fact that this brilliant, indomitable girl who's lost so much and who has so much to live for was made helpless today, until she wasn't, until she found a way to use her voice. I scream for the life she might have been forced to live—a life that looked nothing like the one she wanted for herself—if she had needed an abortion after this bill had passed. I scream as loud as I can just to join my voice with hers, just to be here with her in this, to be a part of this with her.

But I don't *just* scream for Shireen. I look down at the Senate floor, where Wendy Davis is still standing somehow, twelve and a half hours after she said, "I intend to speak for an extended period of time."

Now she's looking up at those of us in the gallery, those of us shouting and screaming and clapping, and she flashes us a peace sign, or maybe it's a V for "Victory." Whatever it is, I scream for her. This whole day started out with Wendy Davis standing up and using her voice to make sure that Shireen, and all the people who had been denied their chance to speak, would finally be heard—and now we're up here returning the favor. I scream for Wendy Davis, because the other team found a way to keep Wendy Davis from speaking for herself even after she put her body on the line for so many hours.

I scream for Shireen, and I scream for Wendy Davis, and I scream for Jesse, too. I scream for my poor, dead friend, who loved getting messed up so much that he made his whole life about getting messed up, and who shot himself up with what he thought was heroin one night because he wanted to find a new way to do it. I never got to say goodbye, or "I'm sorry," or "What the hell is wrong with you," or "Please don't do this," or any of the things I've spent so many months wishing I had been able to say to him, things that I probably wouldn't have found the courage to say back then even if he were still alive, but things that I would for damn sure speak right to his face after today. I imagine for a minute that he's still alive, still sitting in that garage apartment, and I'm going over there at four o'clock in the afternoon, when everybody else is gone, and saying to him, "God damn it, you can be so much more than this," and not leaving until he believes me. But he isn't, and I can't, so I scream instead, wildly and loudly, with everything I have, because I don't have anywhere else to put what I've been feeling except into this scream, and it feels so good just to use my voice. I never would have had the words to change Jesse's mind, but I don't need them now. All I need to do is keep making noise.

So I keep screaming. I look over at the section of people wearing blue, and they're the only quiet group in this room. It's so loud in here that I feel sorry for them, but I'm not going to stop for Cassie or for anybody else. Instead, I scream *for* Cassie, even though she must be so disappointed right now, because I know that the sequence of events that led me to be here right now began when Cassie called me, and Cassie called me because she believed that I was someone good, and I didn't wake up feeling like that was true this morning, but I feel that way now. So I scream for Cassie, my throat raw and getting rawer, because I want her to hear me—not to feel betrayed or let down or disappointed, but to know that I wouldn't have the strength to do this if she hadn't believed in me, and if she hadn't been someone so honest and passionate that I wanted to become someone honest and passionate, too. I see Cassie put her hands over her ears, and I scream for her anyway.

I scream for all of them—for Shireen, and Wendy Davis, and Jesse, and Cassie—and because I have so much more time to go, I scream for Jacob Kohler and Tommy Richman. Those boys might put bricks through my window or beat the hell out of me the next time they see me, but I'm not afraid of them anymore. I'm not ashamed of myself, and I'm not afraid of what'll happen the next time they see me. I scream for them because they're not good people, and so they aren't going to lend their voices to this, and that means that I need to make mine that much louder.

And I scream for myself.

I scream for the person I want to be, and I scream for the person I've been afraid I was. I scream because I want to be someone who demands that people hear him—to be someone who would speak up when Jesse started ruining his life, someone who would tell Jacob and Tommy to go to hell, someone who Cassie Ramirez would recognize as an equal even if we're not on the same side, someone who can stand next to Shireen and deserve to be in the same space, who is worthy of being with her in this. I scream because I remember what Mr. Monaghan told me earlier today—that there are two kinds of men in the world. Well, there are two kinds of *people* in the world, too: the people who are willing to scream when screaming is what's called for, and the people who aren't. And I want to be—I *have to be*—the kind of person who screams. All of the best people I know—Shireen and Cassie and Debbie Monaghan and Mr. Monaghan—are that kind of person, and I've seen what happens to me when I spend my time with the other kind. If I'm not the kind of person who screams, then I'm the kind who will watch my friend head down a path that ends with him dying in the back of an ambulance, the kind who will drive the getaway car for bullies and cowards because he's too afraid not to. So I let my voice go, and I scream and I scream and I scream and I scream, my voice part of a roar that consists of hundreds of voices screaming out our frustrations and our faith and our hopes and our fears and our love. I look around the room, at the faces and the bodies and the mouths of the people who are just like me and not like me at all, and I let my voice have power for the first time in my life.

11:55 pm

But there's still so much time to go. My voice hurts, my hands are sore, my arms are tired from clapping. We're all feeding on the energy in the room, and none of us wants to let anybody down, and so we all keep pushing through. On the Senate floor, all of the senators on our side stare up at us with looks of disbelief. Most of them hold up two fingers for peace or victory or whatever; Kirk Watson has his phone out to take our picture.

Someone channels the formless screams into a chant of "Let her speak!" and we pick that up right away. It feels good to have some rhythm. It feels like the entire room is shaking. I know that the Capitol building is made out of limestone, but I imagine that they can hear us all the way down in the second subbasement.

And it's not just us, either—now that we've shifted to a chant, I can hear more screams, loud and formless and frantic, coming from outside the gallery.

Down on the floor, some senators—even Wendy Davis herself—clap along with us in rhythm. And it feels like *this* is politics, or at least this is democracy. I'm sure it's not a great idea for all decisions about laws and policy to be made by groups of people chanting "Let her speak!" so loudly that the politicians can't hear themselves to vote, but right now, it feels like the only appropriate response. They took Wendy Davis's voice, so we're using ours, instead, to accomplish what she came here to do.

The chant shifts to "Wendy! Wendy! Wendy!" and I join that one, too. Shireen grabs my arm and points to a big clock on the wall that I hadn't noticed before—it reads 11:58, and we are still going strong. On the other side of the gallery, a handful of DPS officers come down the aisles, and one of them puts his hands on a woman in her twenties and leads her to the exit. There are maybe four officers total, and they each take someone and lead them out. It makes me nervous, but I keep shouting—there are just two minutes left on the clock, and if I need to tell my mom that I was arrested tonight because I shouted down our state legislature, at least this time I'll be in trouble for doing something I believe in.

But they're only taking four people at a time, and at that rate, they'll never shut us all up. So we keep the chant up. Shireen and I hold hands and stare at the clock, which keeps right on ticking—and sure enough, those seconds turn into minutes and that minute hand sends the hour hand to the other side of midnight. I look down at the Senate floor, and Wendy Davis points to the clock, which reads 12:01. I pull out my phone, just to double-check, and it says the same thing.

The cheering reaches a new pitch now, and then something weird happens on the floor: Duncan starts taking the vote anyway. It's definitely after midnight, which means that it's definitely June 26, which means that the special legislative session is definitely over. The whole room's cheers and screams turn to another unified chant now, this time of "Shame! Shame! Shame!" and I join that one, too.

I turn around to Josh, since he's a lawyer and seems to know what's happening better than anybody else here. He leans down, and I cup my hands over his ear and shout, "Can they do that?"

He cups his hands over his mouth and shouts, "A hundred forty thousand people just saw the clock! It's over!" As if to echo him, on the floor, Senator West holds up his watch and shouts, "It's after midnight! We can't take the vote after midnight! There's no session!"

After so many close calls, it's hard to believe that we've actually won. But the energy of the room starts to shift as it becomes clear that, whatever is going on, it's not happening on the Senate floor anymore. People start to trickle out of the gallery, and Shireen and I join them.

* * *

The Capitol is a mess of people, all of whom look as worn out as I feel. It's loud as hell out here, too. Shireen and I pass through the buzzing swath of confused, anxious orangeshirts. Nobody seems to know anything, and all the agitation just makes me feel even more exhausted.

"Can we, like, go downstairs or something?" Shireen says, her voice hoarse from the screaming. "I can't take this."

I nod, and we make our way to the crowded stairway and down to the next crowded level. Then down again, and then again. Finally, we find ourselves back in the basement.

It's still busy down here, but less so than the rotunda. Up there, you could barely push past people. Here, there are just pockets of folks moving around, and it's quiet enough to have a conversation.

"Dude," Shireen says. "This is nuts."

I nod. "What happened up there? What's going to happen next?"

"Who knows?" she says. "But like—everything

is nuts. This whole day. You know, you were pretty much the last person I wanted to see this morning."

I nod. "Well, same."

"I've been mad at you for such a long time. But mostly I think I've been mad at myself. And Jesse. And—and everybody." She throws her hands around like she's saying she's mad at the two randos walking past the door to some state representative's office, and probably at whoever that office belongs to as well.

"You aren't the only one who lost all their friends, you know. I haven't even talked to Holly since it happened. I was here by myself because I didn't want to be around anybody anyway. But you showed up. And that means a lot."

"I keep thinking about how if this had happened a year ago, we might all have been here together—you and me and Jesse and Bobby and Holly and everybody else," I say. "It would have been really different."

She shrugs. "Everything was really different a year ago. I think I've changed a lot. We both have. You were kind of a real shit to me sometimes, you know that? Even before you threw a brick through my friggin' window." She says it warmly, more teasing than angry.

"I was," I agree, thinking about being on the balcony with her and resenting her for being nice to me because I wanted to wallow in self-pity and blame her for how I felt.

"I'm not the person I was a year ago," she says, finally. "And I liked being that girl, but she has a lot of regrets. And I'm tired of thinking about her, and I'm tired of being defined by those regrets."

"Yeah," I say. "Boy, do I know what you mean by that. I'm done being the person I was before."

"So the person you are now," she says. "Who do you think he is?"

I look around the Texas State Capitol building at the people in orange still trickling up from E2.002, and then at Shireen, in her homemade "Come and Take It" T-shirt with the neck cut out, and then at my own orange shirt that says "Stand with Texas Women," and I think about what brought us here.

"Somebody who figured out how to stand up for what he believes in," I say. "I wish I had figured that out earlier. I wish I had figured that out when it might have made a difference for Jesse."

Shireen nods and taps her chest, like she wishes the same thing for herself.

"And I really wish I had realized what we could accomplish when we were on the same side," I add. "But I'm glad we figured that out together."

2:14 am

There was nothing for us to do, really, but there was no way we were going to leave until we knew for sure what had happened to the bill. We knew the vote came after midnight, and we knew the whole world watched it happen—but we didn't know if the people who took the vote would care. So Shireen and I just spent the past two hours milling around—looking for leftover pizza, throwing away empty boxes, finding outlets to charge our phones, and checking with every adult who seemed like maybe they would have an answer for us.

"Do you want a ride home?" Shireen asks me now, and I shake my head.

"I'm not sure I'll ever be able to get to sleep," I say. "At least riding my bike home will burn up some of this energy."

We go upstairs. The building is a little less crowded than it was during the height of the filibuster, but the orange army is still very much assembled. We reach the ground floor and see a group of several hundred people, all packed into the rotunda and ready to pass out from exhaustion.

In the middle of the room, a blond lady with a microphone—it's Cecile Richards, the president of Planned Parenthood—is reading a message from her phone.

"This is straight from Senator Wendy Davis," she says, and every set of ears in the place perks up. "She says—'I love you guys.'" There's a big cheer, and shouts of "We love you, too!" from people who apparently didn't blow out their voices two hours ago. Then she goes on. "The lieutenant governor has agreed that the bill is dead."

And then I do find my voice again to join the cheer with everyone else.

"I knew it!" Shireen says. "I *knew* we beat it."

Before I can say anything, Debbie Monaghan— along with her father, who must be downright *pooped* right now—walks by.

"Oh, hey!" she says. "I didn't know y'all were still here."

The crowd splits up, the atmosphere like you'd find at a football game after the home team won big. Debbie and Mr. Monaghan start walking toward the doors. Shireen and I join them, and the four of us walk out of the Capitol together. It's June in Texas, where the heat and the humidity don't dissipate even well after midnight, but the fresh air feels amazing anyway. I break off from the group for a minute to get my bike, then I return to walk the bike through the Capitol grounds and across 15th Street with them.

"So we did it, huh?" I say to them and to anybody else in earshot, just because it feels good to say.

"Yeah," Debbie says. "I mean, for now, anyway. Did you hear what Dewhurst said when he announced that the bill was dead? 'It's been fun. See you soon.'"

I look over at Shireen, confused. "What does that mean?"

Debbie shakes her head. "It means they're probably gonna call another session and force it through in that one."

"That's—they can *do* that?" I stammer.

"Ah, we knew that going in," Mr. Monaghan says. "Today, we won one. That doesn't happen too fuckin' often. Take your victories where you can find 'em, kid. You'll live longer."

I try to wrap my head around this. "So we won, but we lost. Or we're *going* to lose, anyway. Doesn't that make all of this seem kind of like a waste of time?"

"We won a battle," Mr. Monaghan says. "Winning a war takes years, and we've been fighting this one for a long fucking time. You string enough battles together, though, and that's how you win the war.

We'll lose some along the way, too, but you keep fighting."

"Forever?" Shireen asks it like she's checking if she needs to build "keep fighting the war" into her future life plans.

Debbie nods and puts her arm around her dad.

"There are always going to be bad things lurking around the corner," she says. "Whatever it is they might end up doing to you, you can't stop them from happening. But you can find people you trust to help you fight them. And if you find the right people, who the hell knows what impossible things you might be able to do. Today we lost a dozen different times— but we still won. We might lose the next time, but we might win it eventually, too. All I can say is after today, I'm not counting any of us out."

It's the sort of thing I've always wanted to be- lieve—that if you just have the right people at your side, you can do anything. My problem has always been that I haven't known how to figure out who those people are. Shireen's one, though, and maybe someday Cassie and I can be those sorts of friends, too.

But figuring all of that out is enough for right now, so I get on my bike, say my goodbyes, and start pedaling. Before I head north, I do one lap around the Capitol with the late-night summer air blowing through my hair, and as I ride through the Capitol grounds, I let out one more scream, just to let anybody who can hear me know that we were here, we found each other, we'll be back, and we will not yield.

Author's Note

I spent the summer of 2013 at the Texas Capitol, covering the fight over abortion rights for the *Austin Chronicle*. Most of the scenes depicted in this book are things I observed firsthand: The blueshirts and orangeshirts avoiding one another in elevators. The lines queuing around several floors of the rotunda. The endless stacks of pizza boxes in the underground extension. The passion and conviction of those who turned up at the Capitol throughout both of the special sessions to fight for their cause.

I also saw the ways that the fight over abortion rights has been deeply unbalanced, even in the years before the US Supreme Court overturned *Roe v. Wade*. I saw the orange-shirted supporters of abortion rights outnumber the blue-shirted proponents of restrictive laws several times over. I saw lawmakers silence hundreds of people who had shown up to testify with the swing of a gavel and the declaration that their intensely personal stories had grown "repetitive." I heard politicians insist that they had no interest whatsoever in restricting abortion access and react with shock at the suggestion that they had any intention other than to make the procedure marginally safer for patients. And, of course, I saw them step over the rules of the Texas Senate to push through a vote with just a few minutes to go before midnight——only to watch as the people in the room whose voices had been gaveled away a few days earlier took power for themselves, however briefly, using their literal voices to buy a few precious minutes of time to kill the bill.

It should be no secret, if you've finished this book, that I believe that abortion rights are essential to the autonomy, freedom, and dignity we are all owed. But I also know that, while the politicians leading the fight to pass abortion restrictions were often doing so cynically——privately, many of them expressed their frustration that they were spending so much time on an issue they didn't care much about——most of the people who came out to the Capitol dressed in blue, and especially the young people among them, were motivated by beliefs as genuine and ardent as those held by their opponents in orange. In writing this book, I wanted to acknowledge that recognizing the conviction of those we disagree with doesn't mean wavering in our own. Rather, it's the opposite——understanding that those we disagree with are no less impassioned, no less sincere, and no less determined than we are strengthens our convictions and our values by testing and reaffirming them.

As of the summer of 2022 and the overturning of *Roe v. Wade*, politicians no longer need to pretend that the abortion laws they pass exist for any reason other than to limit access to the procedure for those who need it. Accordingly, the laws in much of the country (and especially Texas) are, as of this writing, wildly more restrictive and punitive than anything in the law that Wendy Davis donned her pink sneakers to filibuster in 2013. What this tells us is that the fight for this right continues, and it's likely to continue for years to come, maybe forever. If there's anything I'd like for readers of this book to take away from it, it's that this fight can be joyful and inspiring as well as heartbreaking and unfair, and that sometimes—not always, but sometimes—your voice can shake the foundations of the institutions that seek to take your power away. That'll be true forever, too.

Acknowledgments

Thank you to everyone who was at the Texas State Capitol in June and July of 2013. It felt like I saw everyone I had ever met in Texas at the Capitol that summer, and I will never be able to think about that time without thinking about Jessica Luther, Lindsay Eyth, Andrea Grimes, Carolyn Jones, Jenny Carlson, Devin Person, Katherine Miller, Blake Rocap, and Dan Vaughn.

This is a book about Texas and politics, but it's also a book about high school. Thank you to Jason Simpson, Jim Laczkowski, John Vechey, M. S. Patterson, Jeff Winston, Brian Zaborowski, Rachel Slager, Nate Bohanan, Liz Bohanan Matthews, Art Mayes, and Sherry VerWey for making that time livable.

Thank you to Amy Gentry, Linden Kelder, Victoria Rossi, Paul Stinson, and Alissa Zachary for being an incredibly supportive and insightful writing group. Thank you to Fernando Flores, Kelsey McKinney, Matt McGowan, Nadia Chaudhury, and

Ronin DePrang for advice, encouragement, guidance, and introductions on the way to publication. Thank you to the *Austin Chronicle* and especially Kim Jones for asking me to write about what was going on at the Capitol in the summer of 2013. Thank you to Andrea Valdez and Abby Johnston for giving me the opportunity to follow the story to its end at the Supreme Court, and to *Texas Monthly* for keeping me on this story on beyond Dobbs. Thank you to Meg Gaertner and everyone at Flux for believing in this book.

Thank you to the people and organizations who kept diligent transcripts and video records of everything that was said on the floor of the Texas Senate on the date of the filibuster, especially Ana Mardoll, Counterpath, and the *Texas Tribune*.

Thanks to Jeff Solomon, Tony Presley, R. A. Lopez, Rachel Carreles-Lopez, Rob Jaffe, Charlie Vela, Marc Villarreal, Cindy Garza, Gabriel Grajales, and Donner from Charlie Daniels Death Wish for being such reliably good friends over so many years. Thank you to my mom for being supportive even though I know we don't agree on the issue at the core of this book. Thank you to my dad for always letting me know that he was proud of me; I wish you'd gotten the chance to see this book published and to post about it on Facebook every day for months.

Thanks to Dio for keeping me company while I wrote this, and to Ozzy for recognizing that I often needed a tug-of-war break while I rewrote it. And thank you, of course, to Katherine Craft, for the love, support, and inspiration that make everything seem possible. You're my favorite person, and my favorite writer.

About the Author

Dan Solomon is a journalist based out of Austin, Texas. He's a senior writer at *Texas Monthly*, and his writing has appeared in the *New York Times*, *Vanity Fair*, and *Details*. He covered the HB2 filibuster for the *Austin Chronicle*, where his work was part of the alt-weekly's AAN Award–nominated coverage. Dan lives in Austin, Texas, with his wife and his dog.